ALDERWOOD ORIGINS

I0626547

I

Escaping Alderwood

Chapter One: The Cry Heard Around Alderwood

written by

DEVON CAREY

published by

SHADOW CREEK PUBLISHING

About the Book

It's 1592, England, Mabel Wakefield lives in domestic bliss with her beloved husband John and newborn son Thomas in the remote village of Alderwood, nestled deep within a foreboding forest. But when a simple whisper brands Mabel as a witch, their joyous world shatters in an instant.

Despite a desperate attempt to silence rumours, more damage is done—Mabel's secret ancestral ties to witchcraft have been exposed to the entire village. Condemned by her community, Mabel finds even her devoted John cannot protect her or their baby from the crazed town.

Soon she is utterly alone, her husband sentenced to public execution and her infant son ripped from her arms. As she races desperately through the village searching for Thomas, she witnesses the merciless Constable Harrow himself orchestrating her beloved John's gruesome sacrificial stoning.

Overwhelmed with anguish, she vows to reclaim Thomas, seeing his tiny form suspended in a cage over John upon the execution stage. For she knows the obsessed Harrow will never cease hunting her, the damned daughter of a witch, whose very existence threatens his iron rule. Her only hope is to somehow flee Alderwood forever. But first she must save Thomas, though the entire village now stands against her.

When Mabel is captured and condemned to rot in the dungeon below Alderwood, Harrow's sadistic torment begins. She can hear Thomas's distant cries echoing day and night somewhere within the underground maze. His wavering wails fracture her sanity.

To reclaim her stolen child, she must achieve the impossible and escape the inescapable dungeon maze, outwit Harrow's mind games, and embrace the shadowed Alderwood Forest where unspeakable horrors lurk amidst the ancient oaks.

Can Mabel save Thomas from the dungeon before his haunting cries shatter her mind? Or will rescuing her son come at the ultimate price in the forest?

dedicated to

Tina Kelley

My light in this dark world,

Thank you for helping me with Alderwood from Day 1

About the Author

I'm just Dev.

Www.EscapingAlderwood.Com

Author's Note

Dear Fans,

I'm beyond thrilled to share with you the first entry in the Alderwood Origins series, *Escaping Alderwood: Chapter One - The Cry Heard Around Alderwood*.

Before we begin, it is important to note that since *Escaping Alderwood* takes place in England, this book was written using British English rather than American English, so you will see distinct differences in the spelling of words than you are used to. This creepy saga has been my passion project since the summer of 2023, born from a lifelong love of immersive horror storytelling that elicits all the chills and thrills, from the time I was six years old when I lived in that haunted trailer in Corpus Christi, Texas to even recently in 2019 when I won over ten awards for a screenplay in which I co-wrote entitled *Crossfyre: Chronicles of Gabriel*, written alongside Dan E. Scott and Christan Van Slyke and so many more stories between the years—like *Fearful Symmetry's Volume I: Legion* published in 2021 by Shadow Creek Publishing, and the soon to be released *Flipside, Book 1* from *The Shadow Chronicles* written with my best friend and brother, Kameron Ramos.

As a kid, I was obsessed with the goosebumps that would creep up my arms reading Stephen King, Clive Barker, Dean Koontz, Richard Mattheson, RL Stine, HP Lovecraft and even Rod Serling's *Twilight Zone*. Those authors and creators sparked my imagination and made me realise the power of frightening fiction to transport readers to terrifying new worlds. When the initial kernel of Alderwood first popped in my brain, I knew I'd landed on something special.

Chapter One: The Cry Heard Around Alderwood

It all started while I was noodling around in Unreal Engine, conjuring creepy 3D environments and characters, and playing through the newly remastered Resident Evil 4—which, let's be real, is some grade A nightmare fuel. The game reminded me how much I adored the dark, intricate world built in Elden Ring. I began thinking of how to craft a fresh horror landscape to get lost in.

A tiny, cursed village filled with centuries of secrets began to take shape. Alderwood appeared picturesque on the surface, but I could sense a lurking rot underneath. Alderwood called to me, wanting its origins told. The more I charted its mysterious lore, the more excited I became.

Crafting Alderwood alone would have been maddening. Thankfully, I had the brilliant mind and eagle eye of my editor, and also my beautiful girlfriend, Tina, who constantly scanned for plot holes and helped refine the continuity since the first day we started this project together. She's been a consistent help ever since.

I created Alderwood for you, my beloved fans, to draw you into its haunted ambience just as I was immersed myself. My hope is that you'll be captivated by this first instalment, with Alderwood staying rent-free in your heads long after you've closed the book.

Why stop at the page, though? Like Resident Evil and Goosebumps before it, Alderwood must spread its reach across mediums and formats. This is only the beginning. We currently have an Alderwood mobile game in development, allowing you to navigate the prison maze while avoiding guards, fighting off the accursed and reuniting mother and child. Soon we'll have short-form YouTube videos unveiling Alderwood lore under the hashtag #AlderwoodOrigins. An immersive VR experience that transports you straight into Alderwood's

Chapter One: The Cry Heard Around Alderwood

twisted realm. Perhaps even a big budget video game bringing Alderwood to gruesome, vivid life. The possibilities are endless for this nightmare-fueled franchise.

But expansive, multi-platform worlds require expansive resources. As a solo creator, I can only do so much alone. This is where you come in, dear reader. Consider supporting me on Patreon—it's like buying me bottomless cups of coffee each month, the rocket fuel I need to bring this once-small horrorscape to its maximal potential. Or hey, even just shopping on the Alderwood merch store helps more than you know! With your help, I can fully immerse the world in the petrifying, expansive, multi-sensory terror-verse that is Alderwood.

The origins are already whispering to me from Alderwood's shadowed depths. Let's write the next grisly chapter of this immersive saga together, my friends. The Alderwood Origins are just beginning.

Spine-tinglingly yours,

Devon Carey

Chapter One: The Cry Heard Around Alderwood

Only A Whisper

The remote village of Alderwood sat unnaturally still on this crisp morning in 1592. Nestled deep in the misty English countryside, it was a place lost to time, untouched by invention or progress. Life moved onward in Alderwood at the same unhurried, tedious pace it had for centuries prior. Thatched roof cottages clustered around a muddy village square, their timber frames of wattle and daub plastered with mud and straw. Lazy tendrils of smoke curled from their stone chimneys, only to fade into a light blanket of fog that perpetually shrouded the village. The dirt roads were soaked from yesterday's rain, meandering past deep ruts carved by generations of iron-rimmed wagon wheels. Scruffy sheep, goats, and pigs wandered freely, foraging for scraps.

Oxen with curved horns pulled creaky wooden carts, their heads bowed in resignation. Women in simple coarse linen dresses and caps carried baskets of eggs on hips as they walked to the market, their wooden clogs sinking into the muck with each step. Men worked the damp fields using horse-drawn iron ploughs, tilling the same heavy clay soil their fathers and grandfathers had before them. Flax and hay swayed beneath the muted morning light that filtered through the misty air.

Alderwood clung fiercely to the past and the old ways. Change and progress were viewed with utmost suspicion. The villagers approached life with a primitive mindset, untouched by new ideas or inventions. Gaia, family and hard work were the pillars of their world. Most had never ventured beyond the familiar confines of the village. The impenetrable Alderwood Forest surrounded them and served as both their protection from outsiders, as well as their prison.

Gossip and hearsay were currency that could make or break a reputation in an instant. The village square served as the gallows where public shame punished any who dared step outside Constable Harrow's rigid social order. Quiet rumours of witchcraft festered in the shadows, waiting to condemn the vulnerable. Suspicion ruled every interaction. One whispered rumour of impropriety or abnormal behaviour could turn even lifelong friends into scornful enemies overnight.

Yet on this morning, an aura of harmony consumed the village square. Roosters crowed, echoing between the cottages. The baker swept his front stoop, waving to the butcher opening his shutters across the way. A young boy guided a small herd of goats through the square, whistling cheerfully. Women gathered to chat and fetch water from the well, their laughter mingling with the gurgle of the splashing buckets.

Inside their modest cottages, wives tended to morning chores with a contented air. Their humming mixed with the crackling of hearth fires and the smell of simmering oat porridge. Golden light filtered through small windows, sunshine piercing earthen floors. Out back, maids hung laundry on lines to dry.

Beyond the village, rays of sunlight burned through the morning mist, announcing the arrival of spring. Birds twittered excitedly amongst the oaks edging the forest. Wildflowers pushed up between patches of colourful petals drinking in the warm light.

Alderwood basked in the glow of the spring season, embracing the brief interlude of peace and harmony. Yet even as sunlight dappled the village square and wildflowers pushed up from the thawing earth, a single whisper traversed the wind, rustling between cottages and winding through the market. It was only a whisper. Rumours spread of a witch lurking amongst the villagers, disrupting the tranquillity with unease and suspicion. Though Alderwood clung fiercely to the past, the future always carried uncertainty. This beautiful morning was a fleeting moment of light piercing the gloom. It was but only a whisper before Alderwood once again sailed into darkness.

1: Mabel's Nightmare

Mabel Wakefield paused outside the village bakery, her wicker basket dangling from her arm. She breathed deep, savouring the warm, yeasty aroma of freshly baked bread that made her stomach rumble. As a girl of only seven, she'd walked this very street with her friends, laughing and dreaming about their futures. Now a married woman of nineteen, Mabel's rosy cheeks were lightly smudged with dirt, her long brown hair falling past her shoulders in waves.

Though weary, Mabel's warm brown eyes held a spark of hope. She still loved Alderwood, even as she saw its flaws more clearly with age. She prayed her own son would grow up to experience all the joys of life in Alderwood.

The bakery's worn wooden sign swung in the morning breeze. Inside, the portly baker Edgar could be seen whistling cheerfully as he pulled golden loaves from the brick oven. Mabel smiled, remembering Edgar's booming laugh and propensity for slipping extra buns into her basket as a child.

"Good morning! Out for the day's bread, I see," Edgar called out jovially, waving a flour-dusted hand through the open shop window.

"Good morning, Edgar!" Mabel replied warmly. "Yes, I'll take..."

Her voice trailed off as she noticed Edgar's rosy smile disappear. His friendly eyes narrowed and darted away, dropping his hand abruptly. Without another word, he turned his back on Mabel and busied himself kneading dough.

Mabel stood frozen, confusion and hurt welling up inside her. Edgar had known her family for years. Why this sudden coldness? Before she could react, Celia Dews, a stout matron from the village, aggressively bumped her shoulder as she hurried past, nearly toppling Mabel's basket.

"Watch yourself, girl," Celia muttered without stopping, shooting a glare over her shoulder.

Mabel steadied herself, stunned. First Edgar, now open hostility from Celia? She had done nothing to provoke such contempt. A sick feeling washed over her as she finally noticed what else was off about Alderwood today.

Faces that usually nodded or smiled in neighbourly greetings were now averted with unveiled malice. Instead of wishing her a good morning, people crossed the street to avoid her all together. The warmth of the community had been replaced by a chill wind of ill will blowing through the village.

Mabel's chest tightened anxiously. Without thought, her hand went to the small wooden cross she wore on a cord around her neck, gripping it like a talisman. As she whispered a prayer for understanding, a high-pitched voice rang out.

"Witch!" little Martha Tanner shrieked, pointing a damning finger at Mabel. Martha's mother gasped and yanked the girl away, casting an apologetic glance. But the damage was done.

That single moment roused the villagers from passive avoidance into open aggression. Angry whispers and pointing fingers followed Mabel as she ran home, basket forgotten. Her heartbeat thundered in her ears, keeping time with her pounding feet.

Witch! The accusation echoed in her mind. But why? She was no witch, that was her mother's fate, not hers. She was just an ordinary Gaia-fearing woman, a young wife and a mother, nothing more. What could have sparked this level of loathing against her so quickly? Apprehension filled Mabel's heart as she fled home.

Chapter One: The Cry Heard Around Alderwood

~*~

Mabel burst through the heavy oak door, the worn iron handle clanging loudly against the inner wall of the small cottage she shared with her husband John and their baby son, Thomas. She collapsed into the chair by the hearth, shaking uncontrollably like a scared rabbit fleeing a fox.

John rushed to her side, his ruggedly handsome face etched with fear and concern. Though weathered from long days working the land, his muscular frame moved with a graceful strength. His piercing hazel eyes met Mabel's frightened gaze.

"Mabel, my love, what evil has befallen you?" he asked urgently, clasping her delicate hands in his large, calloused ones. Worry creased his brow as his eyes searched hers intently. With his strong jaw and unkempt black hair, he cut a striking figure even in this dishevelled state. But now fear shadowed his chiselled features. He gave her hands a gentle, reassuring squeeze as he waited for her response.

In a frenzied rush, Mabel described the inexplicable hostility and contempt she had faced that day in their once-friendly village—the suspicious sidelong glances from Edgar, Celia, Abigail, and many more angry whispers behind raised hands; familiar faces had turned cold and accusing for no reason at all. She clutched John's muscular arms as she finished.

"They called me a witch, John!" she cried hysterically, tears streaking her cheeks. "Me! A witch! Why would anyone believe such a horrible lie?"

Deep down, Mabel knew the truth of her lineage, though it was a secret carefully guarded from all. Her mother was *The* Mother Agnes, who had been a powerful witch and fled the village nineteen years ago to protect her newborn child, leaving Mabel to be raised by her father, who was just an ordinary man, Aiden, the town's blacksmith. But now it seemed someone had mysteriously discovered the truth of her buried heritage.

John clasped Mabel against his broad chest, stroking her hair as she wept, attempting to soothe her frayed nerves. His eyes darkened with anger at her mistreatment.

"I don't know who has poisoned minds against you, my love," he vowed fiercely through gritted teeth, "but I swear on my life I will make them pay for this outrageous false accusation."

Mabel gazed up at her staunch defender, drawing courage from the fiery resolve in his eyes.

Just then, the cottage door creaked open. Mabel and John whirled to see a small pale face peering inside, mostly obscured by shadow. It was ten year old Timothy Harrow, Constable Harrow's son.

Timothy was a slight, sickly looking boy with sallow skin that hung off his gaunt frame. His dark, sunken blue eyes peered out from beneath a mop of unwashed blond hair. Though just a child, his eyes gleamed with malevolent purpose far beyond his years. He wore a threadbare tunic that hung limply from his bony shoulders, the hem stained with mud.

"Agnes..." the boy said, drawing out the secret name with sinister relish. His reedy voice echoed in the silence. A smile twisted his pale lips, revealing rotted teeth. The forbidden name hung heavy in the air between them like a curse.

With sudden horrified understanding, John leapt to his feet, grabbed his woodcutting axe from the wall and charged after Timothy into the cool morning air.

Mabel rushed to the foggy window, heartbeat pounding against her ribs. Through the wavy glass pane, she witnessed John catch the boy at the forest's edge. Their angry voices echoed back to the cottage, rising in pitch. John swung the axe, and then swung again, followed by an abrupt silence.

Mabel stood frozen and backed away from the window, hand cupped to her mouth, scarcely daring to breathe. The night pressed in around her, anticipation unending.

After an agonising wait, John returned, his towering frame a silhouette within the rising sun. He staggered up to the cottage. Anguish was carved into his face when he stepped into the dim interior.

Mabel peered through at her husband's hulking silhouette in the doorway sheathed by the blinding sun. She could just make out his grim expression and the limp bundle cradled in his arms. Fresh blood glinting wetly on his hands.

The boy's head lolled to one side in John's arms. A deep gash above Timothy's forehead was the first thing Mabel noticed, eyes vacant and unseeing.

"He left me no choice," John heaved, full of despair. "Somehow the boy learned of your mother."

Mabel stifled a horrified gasp, hands flying to her mouth. Bile rose in her throat as the reality sank in–John had killed Constable Harrow's son. How had Timothy known? She suppressed a shudder, imagining what malevolent spirits may have whispered in the boy's ear, spurring him to reveal forbidden knowledge.

John hid the boy's broken body behind the cottage, under some brush. It was too late. The irreparable damage had been done.

Through the window, Mabel glimpsed little Martha Tanner pointing an accusatory finger at their cottage, her high-pitched child's voice carrying in the wind. "Witch!"

Mabel slammed the wooden shutters closed, her heart pounding. The witch hunt John had sworn to prevent was now inevitable. But she would not flee without Thomas. Mabel's mind raced as she tried to make sense of it all. Her mother had fled years ago to protect her from the stain of her witch's ancestry. At the time, it had seemed a noble sacrifice. But now, with Mabel's secret exposed, it appeared to be for naught. Though Agnes had tried to save her from this fate, witchblood still flowed through her veins.

And now… the entire village knew–her mother's exile had only delayed the inevitable reckoning. Why hadn't Agnes stayed? Together they could have tried to rally the villagers to their cause. Or at least faced the pyre side-by-side, mother and daughter together until the end.

But instead, Agnes had abandoned her, left her alone to confront the vicious lies and superstitions that consumed Alderwood to its rotten core.

Mabel's hands clenched into fists.

There would be time later to curse Mother Agnes for putting her in this position, but for now—she had to focus on saving Thomas.

"Thomas!" Mabel cried out, rushing to cradle him in her arms. As she held him close, her mind raced with fears about the mob that could arrive at any moment. She trembled at the thought of the cruelty the villagers could inflict on her child. Would they rip him from her arms? Hurl stones and accusations? The terror of the unknown gripped her heart. Tears streamed down her cheeks as she pressed desperate kisses to Thomas' forehead. She had to protect her baby at all cost, even if it meant fleeing into the Alderwood Forest. He was all that mattered now.

John dropped a heavy oak beam across the front door to bar it and returned to Mabel, "You must go," he urged in a stern tone. "Take Thomas and escape Alderwood before the mob arrives!"

Mabel knew he spoke the truth. With tears in her eyes, she hurried to the backdoor as John screamed, "Go now. Get out of Alderwood!"

A deafening smash stopped Mabel's hand before it could even touch the handle of the backdoor. The door burst inward, revealing a dishevelled young woman falling into the room. "Mabel, it's me!" the woman cried in a hoarse yet familiar voice.

Mabel gasped as she recognized the filthy figure–it was her childhood friend Rebecca Crawford. Though her bright blue eyes were now dimmed with fear, Mabel knew her instantly.

"They're coming for you!" Rebecca warned urgently. "Constable Harrow leads the mob, they'll be here any moment!"

From outside came the roar of the mob, and in an instant the front door shuddered under a barrage of fists.

Mabel's eyes widened in terror. Her heart pounded wildly in her chest like a caged bird. "We're surrounded!" she screamed, panic gripping her voice.

She wrapped her arms around Thomas, pressing him close, tears streaming down her face. She kissed his head, whispering, soothing words, willing her touch and voice to cast out his fear. His panicked cries slowly subsided as he nestled into her warmth.

John gripped his axe with grim resolution, his strong jaw set. "Go!" he bellowed over the din. "Take our boy and flee! I'll hold off the mob!" He left no room for argument.

Rebecca grasped Mabel's arm, eyes pleading for forgiveness. "Whatever happens, don't look back," she urged. "Just keep running!" Her final words were drowned out by the splintering of wood as the mob broke through the front door.

Mabel fled out of the cottage, the sun beating down on her. From the distance she heard Constable Harrow cry out in fathomless grief.

"No!" Harrow's voice thundered, saturated with black rage having found his son's body behind the cottage. Despite her fear, Mabel felt a stab of remorse for his loss. But survival for her and her own child drove her onward.

Branches tore at her dress and hair as she ran. Thomas wailed, alerting all to their flight. Somewhere behind them John battled the deranged villagers, his shouts rising over the thud of his axe and the cries of the mob.

A grasping hand shot from the shadows, stopping Mabel short. She stumbled, losing her grip on Thomas. The mob descended like a pack of Alderwolves, their gnarled hands tearing the wailing babe from her arms.

"No!" Mabel screamed, but it was too late. Thomas was swallowed by the dark mass of twisted faces, disappearing into the chaos, before she could even get to the edge of the Alderwood Forest.

Mabel was clubbed brutally from behind. A lightning bolt of pain exploded in her skull. Her vision flickered, legs crumbling beneath her as she was knocked unconscious.

~*~

Time slowed and blurred. It was dusk by the time she finally drifted back to consciousness. She found herself lying in a muddy ditch concealed by roadside brush. She touched her throbbing head and her fingers came away slick with blood.

Two small crimson eyes watched from the forest's edge, but they vanished in an instant. Some unknown ally must have dragged her body there to hide her from the mob's wrath. Was it Rebecca who had moved her to safety? She wasn't sure.

Where had the mob taken her babe?

Mabel's head spun as she struggled to rise, legs unsteady, shaking with a cold chill. In the distance, the hateful clamour of the mob echoed through the early night, rising from the village square.

Chapter One: The Cry Heard Around Alderwood

She had to get closer. Had to find Thomas and somehow save him from the deranged throng. Her heart hammered a frantic rhythm against her bruised ribs.

Disoriented but driven by desperate determination, Mabel staggered through Alderwood's narrow back alleys. She stuck to the shadows, the moon–becoming her sole companion. Debris littered the cramped passages–broken barrels, piles of foul rags, even a bloated rat corpse with milky dead eyes. With every step the stench of rotting garbage assaulted her nose, threatening to turn her stomach. But she pressed on, focused only on the distant cries of her stolen child.

As Mabel reached the edge of the village square, she hesitated. Dread washed over her. The hateful clamour of the village was louder now, raised in frightening frenzy. Her heart dropped into her stomach when she realised what they were chanting.

"Stone him! Stone him!"

Peering around the alley's corner, the horrific scene exploded before Mabel's eyes. In the torchlight, a sea of crazed faces surrounded a raised wooden platform in the centre of the square. On it, her beloved John was bound and hunched–battered, bleeding, with stones piled high behind him. Fresh bruises mottled his skin.

Beside him stood Constable Harrow, coordinating the execution. The 55-year old's cruel blue eyes glinted from beneath the shadow of his wide-brimmed black hat. His sharp features were framed by short silver-streaked black hair and a cleanly shaven face.

Above them swung a crude iron cage, suspended from a gnarled tree limb by ropes. Inside, Thomas wailed in terror, his face contorted in anguish. His tiny hands clung to the bars as the cage swung over the execution stage like a pendulum.

The ritual continued, each crushing stone a blood-chilling, deliberate countdown towards John's death. She clutched the alley wall as if it were the only thing keeping her upright.

Constable Harrow heaved two more massive stones from the pile, dropping them onto John's back in quick succession. John's pained gasp pierced the frenzied air as the weight crushed his ribs, his face contorting in agony. Every sinew in his body strained against the torture inflicted by the Constable.

Three stones now lay piled upon him. His proud posture sagged, his head hanging defeated. Vision blurring with tears, Mabel released her grip on the alley wall. She had to reach Thomas before it was too late. She couldn't do anything for John right now, but there was still hope for their son.

Constable Harrow dropped the fourth stone. John's haunting moans of agony tangled with the shrill cries of Thomas in the cage.

From the crowd, Elderly Abigail emerged from the shadows and began operating the cage's lever now that the Seven Stone Ritual was almost over.

The weight of the stones threatened to crush the life from John's body. Mabel's pulse raced, her entire soul crushed. Her husband's unending torment mixed with her son's frightened cries was more than her heart could bear.

As the fifth stone crashed down, John let out a guttural scream unlike any sound Mabel had heard before. His back bowed under the massive weight as his body futilely fought against being snapped in half.

Mabel could see the agony etched in his face. His dying eyes met hers, filled with searing pain and desperate regret that he could not save her or their son.

The sixth stone slammed down and John's body convulsed, blood spewing from his mouth. Mabel cried out, reaching towards him even as the mob pressed in tighter around her, cutting off any hope. She clawed against them like a caged animal, "Get off me! John!"

Abigail's grip stayed steady on the lever. With each slow, ominous click, she lowered Thomas further, the cage inching closer to the grasping hands of the crazed horde. Time was running out.

Mabel knew she could not save John. But she would be damned if she let them take Thomas, too. With a feral scream born of fear and rage, she shoved through the throng and revealed herself.

"Witch!" Constable Harrow's voice bellowed above the madness. But to Mabel his shouts were muted, insignificant. Her universe narrowed to only Thomas, his little face red and damp with tears, tiny hands still grasping the bars in angst.

"Mama's coming, Thomas!" Mabel slammed into Abigail, shoved her aside and seized the lever to finish lowering the cage.

For only a moment, Mabel was free to wrench open the cage door and pull Thomas into her arms, breathing in his sweet baby scent. Her baby boy trembled against her heaving chest.

Brutish hands seized Mabel, ripped her back by the shoulders and knocked her to the ground, Thomas still glued to her bosom. Crazed faces she once knew surrounded her in savage fury. "The witch has the child!"

they cried. Constable Harrow thundered toward her, face contorting with rage and betrayal.

They ripped Thomas from her grasp. As her babe wailed, terrified, Mabel screamed and clawed against them with the ferocity of a mother bear defending her cub. But it was no use–Thomas disappeared back into the throng.

Abigail accepted Thomas gently from the grasping hands and held onto him like he was her own. Mabel collapsed, sobbing and broken. Harrow loomed above her, his cold voice chilling her to the bone. "Your husband murdered my boy. Now it's time for Gaia to judge his blackened soul."

Harrow walked up on the stage and picked up the seventh stone and hoisted it high above his own head, eight feet above John's body already under six hundred pounds of pressure.

"Please, no!" Mabel screamed, reaching with a weak hand toward her beloved.

The stone fell, crushing the last breath of life out from John's lips.

"Throw the witch in the dungeon!" Constable Harrow roared, ripping away the wooden cross from around her neck.

The mob echoed the Constable's excitement in bloodthirsty triumph. Prison guards dragged her away from the stage where John lay flattened beneath the seven stones.

No saviour emerged from the town of Alderwood, not a single friend or family member was on her side. Mabel's eyes begged and pleaded toward Edgar, darting next toward Celia. Nothing. Rebecca was nowhere in sight, either. She had probably fled through the forest after warning her. Not even her own father was there. She thought that her father of all people would have defended her and been by her side in her hour of need.

Curse you, father! Coward!

The mob followed as she was being dragged down the path toward the Alderwood Jail, crying "Witch!" and hurling foul insults. Rotten vegetables and stones pelted her enroute to the dungeon. She blinked through hot tears.

Ahead loomed the gaping gates of the courtyard–and beyond that, the hulking stone façade of the Alderwood Jail, like the craw of a beast waiting to swallow her whole. She was hauled through the imposing gates into a central courtyard surrounded by high stone walls. Flickering torchlight illuminated chains hanging menacingly on the walls leading down to a shadowy stone staircase.

With each step, the moon ascended higher. The entrance of the Jail swallowed her. She whipped her head around, catching one final glimpse of her sweet babe's face from so far away, still cradled in the arms of Elderly Abigail.

Then there was nothing.

As they entered the dungeon, a prison guard seized Mabel and shoved a burlap bag reeking of rot over her head. Musty darkness swallowed her, the rough material scratching her face.

The only sound she could still hear was the shrill, distressed cries of her babe and the triumphant cheers coming from the villagers on the surface. Thomas' wails grew fainter and more distant as Mabel was dragged deeper through the dungeon maze filled with unexplainable horrors that she had only heard about in Origin stories.

The air grew thicker with mould, mildew and hopelessness. Her footsteps echoed off the stone walls as she was led blindly to her own cell. Heavy oak and iron groaned as the door creaked open. She was shoved inside onto the dirty floor, the smell and taste of filth filling her mouth. Behind her, the door slammed shut with a resounding clang that reverberated through her bones.

She pulled the burlap bag off her head and took in her bleak surroundings. The cell was enveloped in darkness, with only thin shafts of moonlight coming through a barred window on the ceiling.

Dripping moisture, scattering cockroaches, gnawed bones in the corner–this would be her tomb. From above she heard nothing, not even a peep or a whimper from Thomas.

Silence settled like a shroud. She buried her face in filthy hands and wept. The image of Thomas remained seared in her mind, his cries echoing all around her in her dungeon cell. She clung to the memory of his loving face, using it as a lifeline to help keep what little hope she still had alive.

For him, she could not despair. However long she remained entombed here, she would find a way back to him. She swore it on her soul–nothing would stop her from saving him.

Surely, Agnes' blood flowed through her veins, though it had lain dormant since her birth. Now she thought she felt it stirring from somewhere deep within her soul, rising like a phoenix from the ashes. She would tap into her power. She would escape this inescapable dungeon maze and reclaim her child. They would flee Alderwood forever, leaving its backward zealotry behind. She and Thomas would forge a new life somewhere they could be accepted and free.

Somewhere far, far away from Alderwood and Constable Harrow's social order.

Escaping Alderwood with her babe... Mabel's first dream.

2: The Awakening

Huddled in the fathomless blackness of her dungeon cell, the icy stones leached away the warmth from her bones. Foul grey water dripped down the grime-slicked walls with a reeking stench of century-old misery. The rough-hewn floor was scattered with filthy straw that did little to cut the chill seeping from the dirt packed stones beneath. This lightless abyss, her tomb, a timeless loneliness swallowed her whole beyond the gnawing ache of endless darkness.

Shadows danced in the faint shafts of moonlight slanting through the barred window overhead on the ceiling. Mabel's wide brown eyes strained for any sign of movement. The rotting body of a dead rodent lay in one corner, crawling with wriggling maggots. Beetles and cockroaches skittered through the rank straw, their scuttling magnified in the dead silence. She could hear the faint scurry and squeaks of live rats in some forgotten crevice nearby. Every sound made her pulse jump, wondering if the blood would get their attention, causing them to venture out and bite at her filthy bare feet.

In her madness, Mabel fancied she could see leering faces twisting out of the grime, mocking her, or maybe it was the Accursed watching her from the walls. The Accursed were people who died in Alderwood and resurrected as an Accursed Origin, stuck between life and death in the state in which they initially died. The Accursed were commonplace closer to the Mainland of Alderwood and out toward the Black Marsh.

Her nails were shredded and caked with blood from clawing manically at the unyielding stones, driven by a manic desperation to dig through to her son. But it was useless–the dungeon walls were five feet thick if they were an inch. She scratched and scrambled like a trapped animal until she collapsed in exhaustion, the cold stones sucking away even the tiniest bit of energy that remained.

When she managed to drift into fitful sleep, Mabel's dreams always began the same–holding Thomas in her arms, gazing down at him as he giggled and cooed. She would hold him close, breathing in his scent, and a feeling of peace would envelop her.

But the dreams would quickly turn dark. His face would contort into a gaping gullet, spewing out spiders, roaches, and beetles. His giggles morphed into demented shrieks as more vermin poured out, hundreds of tiny legs spewing from his gaping jaws.

Mabel would try to drop him in revulsion, only to find her arms frozen, forced to hold his wriggling body tighter as it changed. Milky, dead eyes pushed out by the mass of spiders, leaving nothing but two black hollow holes looking back at her, accusing her for his fate.

Meanwhile Constable Harrow loomed behind her, features twisted in malevolent glee. "This is your legacy, witch," he would rasp as spiders flowed down his arms like a black prickling waterfall. "The boy bears your tainted blood."

Mabel screamed and thrashed, but could not wake from the nightmare as Thomas' body burst open, releasing a tsunami of cockroaches that washed over her in a tidal wave. They skittered across her skin, hundreds of tiny legs probing and biting as she sobbed in horror and self-loathing.

Only when the last of the scampering vermin had disappeared down her mouth in the dream, causing her to choke, would Mabel finally jerk awake, gagging and clawing desperately at her throat. She would thrash around on the floor, still feeling hundreds of tiny insect legs crawling all over her clammy skin, probing and biting at her flesh.

Chapter One: The Cry Heard Around Alderwood

Her tattered nails raked angrily across her arms and face, drawing blood in her frenzy to rid herself of the phantom sensations. But it was no use—the feeling of being blanketed by roaches and spiders persisted long after waking.

Mabel retched drily, vomiting bile as she imagined those same crawlers churning inside her belly. She swiped at her mouth with the back of a trembling hand, rationally afraid she would glimpse an insect leg protruding from between her lips.

Only after what felt like hours of gagging, spitting, and swatting manically at her body did the phantom sensations fade. When Mabel finally managed to catch her breath, the rank chill of the cell greeted her once more. A draft whistled through the window overhead, carrying with it the stench of decay.

As she shivered on the floor, a shadow passed from above. She gasped and looked up to see Timothy's ghastly face pressed against the bars, peering down with pale, dead eyes. Rotting flesh hung off his skull in strips, maggots writhing in the crevices. But even more horrific were the unmistakable axe wounds that had ended his life. Mabel shuddered as she took in the deep gash across his forehead, nearly cleaving his head in two. Shredded flaps of skin framed the mortal blow. Her eyes trailed lower, widening at the chunks of flesh ripped from his shoulder, sinew and bone exposed. She recalled John's powerful swings of the axe that had delivered each killing strike.

Timothy's cold gaze bore into her soul, a hollow set of eyes looking through her. His rotted jaws unhinged in a silent scream, dagger-like teeth glinting wetly in the moonlight.

Mabel scrambled back, hyperventilating, as the Accursed clawed through the bars. She could almost feel its frigid, foetid breath on her face as it tried to bite through attempting to reach her.

The Accursed lingered at the window a moment longer before fading back into the gloom, leaving Mabel panting and shaking on the floor.

She had once prayed for rain, but now feared what fell from the heavens more than dying of thirst. For each day in this abyss eroded her grasp on reality and brought her closer to a predictable end. Just one more lost soul amongst the Accursed Origins of Alderwood.

She shuddered, imagining her beloved John's gentle face distorted into a hideous form.

What had they done with his body after the execution? Did it lie in an unmarked grave, or had they desecrated it further, leaving it to rot where it fell? Bile rose in her throat as she pictured John's strong form bloated and ravaged, swarming with maggots like the rats in her cell.

Unless... a dark notion crept into her thoughts. Had they burned his body, like they did for witches? That was the only way to prevent the dead from rising as one of the Accursed.

Mabel's stomach flipped at the thought of John's body reduced to ashes. It would be better than an eternity spent prowling Alderwood in undeath.

She imagined those gentle eyes that had gazed at her with such warmth now sunken and lifeless. It would break Mabel's spirit to see her beloved cursed to haunt Alderwood as punishment for crimes he did not commit.

Except, he did commit a crime. The murder of Timothy Harrow…

Because of my mother! He was only trying to protect me…

Mabel clung to the hope that John had escaped such a wretched fate. She whispered prayers into the emptiness of her cell, hoping that his soul had found some solace, untainted by the ancient evil that infested this place. For if anyone deserved eternal peace, it was John. Not endless unrest…

Each time Mabel jerked awake, it took longer for her to shake off the nightmares. She feared she was sliding into permanent madness, with no way to escape this insane cycle of damnation.

~*~

On the seventh night, the heavy door to Mabel's cell groaned open. She cringed back like a feral animal, shielding her eyes, as blinding torchlight fell across the floor like an outstretched hand.

A hulking silhouette filled the threshold. Seven foot tall Constable Harrow ducked under the low lintel as he stepped forward. The flickering torch flames threw his chiselled features into sharp relief; this had been the first real look Mabel had given the old man since she had watched him kill John.

Though aged, Harrow cut an imposing figure. As Alderwood's lawmaker, the power he wielded showed in the set of his broad shoulders and stern blue eyes. Once, long ago when Mabel was but a child, they had been friends. She vividly recalled toddling after him as he patrolled the village, gazing up in wide-eyed awe at the tall

"Guardian of Alderwood" as she had known him growing up.

But those innocent days were distant memories now. Any warmth or compassion he once held for her had turned to resentment as he blamed her family for his only son's death. His grief warped into a dark vendetta against her, erasing any remnants of friendship. Now she cowered before Harrow like a cornered animal, knowing he would show her no mercy.

He started with, "So witch, have you settled into your new accommodations?"

Mabel scrambled forward on hands and knees. "Please, let me see my boy!"

Harrow stepped forward, features thrown into sharp relief by the torch flames, carrying a tin plate slopped with greasy gruel and rotting meat scraps.

The rancid odour hit Mabel's nostrils, making her dizzy with hunger. She vaguely remembered her last proper meal–had it been the rabbit stew and hard bread the night before the mob came? An eternity ago. Since then she'd survived on scraps scrounged from the fouled straw and drank from a cornered tin bowl–tainted from rat shit daily that she had to constantly finger out–that she continued filling with rain water when it came in through the ceiling's window.

Unfortunately, due to the lack of rain, she had run out of drinkable water three days ago.

Now her vision tunnelled, fixated on the first real food she'd seen in ages—even if it was foetid gruel crawling with maggots. Mabel's empty stomach clenched painfully, her mouth filling with unexpected saliva. She would've killed for a sip of water to ease her raw throat, parched from days of screaming and crying. Rain. Soon. Please.

"You'll not lay eyes on him again, witch," Harrow said coldly, dropping the plate. Food splattered across the floor.

Mabel fell upon the mess, scooping up chunks of spoiled meat, cramming it into her mouth. She gagged at the taste but forced herself to swallow every morsel, even licking the grime clean from the stones afterward.

Harrow's lip curled in disgust at this creature before him—this woman he'd once called friend—devoured rotten garbage like an animal. "I should whip you bloody and leave you to rot for what your wicked family has done," he continued once she had swallowed the last scrap. "But hearing your bastard child's cries will keep you tethered here until dementia takes your feeble mind."

Mabel barely heard him over the pounding of her pulse as blessed nutrition, however rotten, finally entered her wasted body. She would've eaten her own filth just to fill her shrivelled stomach. Harrow might degrade her humanity, but he could not defeat a mother's spirit sustained by the dream of holding her son again one day.

She sprang up with sudden feral intensity, fingers curled into claws, teeth bared. Harrow stepped back despite himself before regaining composure.

"If you dare touch the boy, I'll rip your throat out with my teeth!" she screeched, flecks of spittle flying from her lips onto Harrow's uniform. She knew it was an empty threat but couldn't stop the words.

Harrow flushed with rage, blue eyes bulging. "You are far beneath me, witch. I should have let them tear you limb from limb for your heresy. Only by the mercy of our beloved Gaia do you still draw breath."

He turned, slammed the door shut behind him and severed the torchflame's light from her cell. Mabel collapsed in despair. Harrow's bootsteps faded, and Thomas kept crying to no end.

Alone in the dark again, she held herself, cried and rocked back and forth in the corner of her cell as her time was guided by vivid flashbacks of a better past.

~*~

Mabel Wakefield, now a young woman of twelve, just married to her beloved John of fifteen. He had crafted a formidable longbow for her nearly as tall as her petite frame. The dried yellowish heartwood formed the compact centre, while supple cream-coloured sapwood made up the outer limbs that flexed with each shot. John had carefully shaped and smoothed the yew wood, steam bending the limbs to create just the right amount of tension. The grip was wrapped in soft leather for comfort, the string woven from sturdy hemp.

Intricate carvings of ivy vines and roses adorned the limbs, detailing John's patient handiwork. When held upright, it was like a staff of power ready to unleash an arrow with deadly force. Yet now it rested gently across Mabel's slender arms as John stood behind her, guiding her hands into position.

"Steady now, my love," John said gently, his strong hands positioning hers properly on the grip. "Take a deep breath and focus. You can do this." She inhaled slowly, cherishing his closeness. She narrowed her eyes at the bundle of hay across the meadow they had set up as a target. The simple brown heap contrasted with the vivid green grasses swaying around it.

With John's patient guidance, she drew back the bowstring, feeling the tension increase in her arms as the flexible limbs bent. The string dug into her fingers, the arrows in her quiver ready. "That's it, nice and steady," he murmured near her ear. His calm voice soothed any nerves. She released the arrow and it whizzed through the air, striking the outer edge of the bale with a satisfying thud.

"I did it!" she cried out in delight and pride. She turned to see John's handsome face smiling tenderly. He wrapped his arms around her from behind in an affectionate embrace.

"With more practice, you'll hit the bullseye every time. I'm so proud of you, my darling wife," he said, nuzzling her neck.

Mabel cherished his warm praise, loving him more with each passing day. "I can't wait to train again tomorrow," she said brightly. "Maybe someday I'll even be as good a shot as you!"

He chuckled and kissed her cheek. "I have no doubt of that, my love."

~*~

In an instant, she saw it all again—John battered and bleeding on the wooden platform, surrounded by the crazed villagers. His wrists were raw and bloody from fighting against the ropes binding him. Fresh bruises and cuts mottled his bare skin as he hunched over in defeat.

Constable Harrow dropped two more stones in quick succession. John screamed, his posture sagged further, chin dropping to his chest as his ribs shattered through his skin.

Tears blurred her vision. She had to reach Thomas before it was too late. Above John, their son wailed in fright within the iron cage suspended above the execution stage.

Her pulse raced as Thomas' panicked cries mingled with John's tortured moans. She felt utterly helpless watching her family's torment play out before her eyes. When the fifth heavy stone crashed down, a guttural scream tore from John's throat. She saw his face contort in raw agony as his back bowed even deeper under the crushing load.

As John convulsed beneath the sixth stone, Mabel screamed his name, clawing through the crowd toward the platform. She met John's desperate, regret-filled eyes moments before the last stone fell.

A broken wail erupted from deep within her soul as his arched body sagged disgustingly deep under six individual hundred pound stones. The prison guards seized her, wrenching her away from the platform's edge. She collapsed, sobbing and broken, as Harrow's cold voice condemned her family followed by the seventh and final stone that ended his life.

Throw the witch in the dungeon!

The horrific memories refused to release their grip on her mind. She dug her nails into her temples, wishing she could tear the images away forever. But Thomas' faint cries echoed down the dungeon corridors entwining with the vivid flashbacks.

Though the visions tortured her, Mabel clung to memories of John's strength and love. For Thomas, she had to channel that same persevering spirit. "We'll be a family again," she whispered, rocking herself to sleep. She would endure this nightmare for her son. "Only for a while," she kept telling herself.

No matter how deeply Harrow buried her, she swore she would never stop fighting to hold Thomas again. She had to keep clawing towards their future as a family. John would want her to stay strong for their son.

The horrible memories subsided for a time, but they lurked–waiting to ambush Mabel's fragile psyche when she least expected it.

~*~

The slivers of daylight that crept through the window were Mabel's only indication of the passage of time in the darkness. These brief moments of illumination melded into the endless nights, creating an abyssal purgatory of maddening uncertainty. Her only solace was marking the transition between day and night on the weeping wall with a pebble she had found in a chipped crevice.

Weeks, months, or perhaps an eternity had passed since she was captured and thrown into isolation, where the stark contrast of fleeting light and impossible darkness consumed her reality.

By now, solitude had become too familiar. No one came except for the occasional visit from Harrow to play disgusting games with her, and the silent guards who irregularly shoved meagre handfuls of rotting food through the slot in her cell door. Mabel's only constant company was the rodents and cockroaches that shared the cell. Around her feet, their skittering magnified in the silence.

Every squeak and scuttle startled her. She imagined them crawling all over her as she slept.

The window above remained Mabel's only link to the outside world. Dim shafts of grey light slanted across the floor at odd hours, partially obscured by the silhouettes of rats. When it rained, she could fill her tin bowl with water to briefly quench her thirst. But the sky had been mercilessly clear for an eternity now, leaving her throat so parched it split and bled when she tried to swallow.

Mabel's mind oscillated between utter despondency and fits of hysterical madness, occasionally cradling a bloated rat because she thought it was Thomas. Ruthless visions of John's execution haunted her, his dying eyes begging for forgiveness. Her filth-caked nails raked crimson furrows across her face and arms as she tried to claw the scenes away.

Then one shadowy night in particular, a terrible silence fell over the dungeon. Thomas was quiet. His cries had ceased altogether. Mabel's pulse roared in her ears. Had Harrow finally taken Thomas away forever? She shrieked until she tasted iron, pounding the cell door with clenched fists.

Silence answered.

An eternity of dread later, the door creaked open. Mabel cringed back as heavy boots thudded over the threshold and into her cell.

Harrow's harsh voice pierced the gloom. Once again he held a plate of rotting, maggot-ridden meat scraps and bones.

"Still alive, witch?" he smirked. "Eat up then."

Mabel's stomach cramped at the smell. She fell upon the slop like an Alderwolf, desperately swallowing every foul morsel as Harrow looked down on her in disgust. When she had licked the plate clean, he slammed the door shut without another word, leaving her weeping in the dark again.

This sadistic ritual repeated sporadically. Whenever she heard Harrow's approaching footsteps, her heart clenched tightly with contradictory spikes of fear, revulsion and irrational hope. A part of her prayed he had finally come to end her misery and let her see Thomas one last time. She recoiled from the malice in his eyes, reminding herself that not a shred of human compassion lingered in this man she had once called friend.

It was clear now that he found pleasure in her suffering. He sought to push her mind into an abyss of misery. She never knew which meal would be her last.

Once, after an eternity of silence, Harrow appeared and stood in the open doorway, gazing down at her in revulsion. Her pulse quickened. Was he finally releasing her from this hell? She staggered forward pleading for mercy. But his mouth only twisted into a monstrous grin. With deliberate, agonising slowness, he pulled the heavy door shut again. Mabel screamed, collapsing to the floor as Harrow's footsteps faded away.

She soon came to welcome the increasingly grotesque nightmares of Thomas, at least she could still see his sweet face in her mind rather than just hearing him cry for her down the hall. The visions fueled her descent into madness. Mabel's nails were shredded, broken quills embedded with blood and skin as she tore relentlessly at the unfeeling stones, screeching Thomas' name over and over again until she could produce only a defeated whisper, "Thomas…"

Chapter One: The Cry Heard Around Alderwood

~*~

The heavy door groaned open. Two prison guards entered cautiously, one holding a torch while the other carried a wooden bowl of watery gruel. Mabel crouched in the far corner, her matted hair falling over her face. She tracked their movement with feral eyes as they approached.

The guard with the gruel set it on the floor and gave it a dismissive shove in her direction. The lumpy beige mush spilled over the side of the bowl, seeping into the hay strewn across the cell floor.

"Eat up, witch," the torch-bearing guard sneered. His companion laughed cruelly. Neither made a move to leave just yet.

Mabel remained motionless, her breathing slow and steady despite her hammering heart. She focused on the shifting shadows cast across the guards' faces by the torch light. The flames lent their features a demonic cast, all harsh angles and leering eyes.

"She don't look so scary now, eh?" the first guard grunted, emboldened by her stillness. He took a step closer, craning his neck to peer under her hair to get a better look at her. "Nothing but a filthy, half-starved wench."

His comrade shook his head nervously, hanging back by the cell door. "Careful fool, she'll put a curse on you." But the arrogant guard ignored him, crouching down to shove the bowl of gruel right under Mabel's face.

"Eat up!" he barked. Before he could react, she erupted upwards, her fingernails raking across his face in ragged furrows. He howled in pain, reeling back with hands clutched to his bloodied cheeks.

Mabel sprang at him in a frenzy, knocking the torch from his grasp. She bore him to the ground, her teeth tearing at his ear like an Alderwolf. He wailed and thrashed beneath her slender frame, unable to match her sudden feral strength.

The other guard leapt into action, scrambling to pull her off his fellow. But she whirled with snarling intensity, her nails clawing at his throat. He stumbled back, calling for reinforcements.

The injured guard managed to land a blow across her jaw, stunning her long enough for him to regain his footing. She crouched, circling them warily as blood dripped from her mouth. The two men brandished clubs defensively, wisely keeping their distance now.

Heavy boots pounded down the hall as more guards arrived. Mabel scuttled back to her corner, glaring at them from its shadows. The newcomers helped drag their wounded comrade out the door before slamming it shut behind them, leaving only faint moans and curses trailing down the corridors.

In the silence that followed, Mabel tentatively licked her split lip, savouring the tang of blood on her tongue. A ruthless satisfaction flowed through her veins, fueled by the guards' suffering and fear. For the first time since being imprisoned, she felt a shred of control, a hint of power in this cruel place. She may be caged, but they now knew she was not yet broken.

The guards kept their distance when depositing Mabel's meals after that, wary of further violence from her. Their fear provided her only sense of agency in this prolonged torment. The void between their brief visits gaped like an eternal grave, threatening to swallow her mind. Harrow fragmented her psyche, with no intention of permitting her escape from this waking hell.

Her only talisman against utter madness was picturing her revenge against him. She nurtured this thought like a glowing ember in the darkness, clinging to it as steadily as she now clung to her hatred. It was all Mabel had left. A relentless obsession took root deep within her, its tendrils strangling any remnants of the gentle soul she once was. She would make Harrow suffer as she had suffered. She would bathe in his blood and feast on his pain.

Harrow had weaponized Mabel's love for her child into a tool to break her, but she refused to yield. Thoughts of Thomas were her beacon of light in this abyss, the sole reason for her continued survival. She pictured Thomas's face again and again, using it to fuel her determination.

Never surrender. Never break. For Thomas.

Another night had come and with it a new dream emerged, Mabel dreamed of her mother. Unlike her usual nightmares of Thomas, this vision held an ethereal beauty.

In the dungeon's dimness, Mother Agnes brightened the cell with an otherworldly radiance. Her silver hair cascaded like a waterfall, with shimmering flowers harvested from the depths of midnight fields. Her kind brown eyes mirrored Mabel's own gaze.A raven with piercing white alabaster eyes perched atop Agnes' shoulder.

It let out a harsh cry, as if sensing something amiss. Before Mabel could react, the raven spread its wings and flew away, disappearing through the window into the night.

Draped in an alabaster robe accented with rich purple arcane symbols embroidered in silver, Agnes looked regal. An intricately carved raven's claw talisman rested upon her slender neck, its presence echoing the ancient might contained within that had been passed down through generations from powerful sorcerers of yore.

"My daughter..." Agnes fractured the silence.

"What now?" Mabel snapped, her voice breaking as she questioned the phantom words. After endless days and nights of pure hell, she no longer trusted even her own sanity. That trust was gone.

Mabel's heart seized with a fragile hope as she strained to see the one who disguised herself as the legendary Enchantress of Alderwood. What if this truly was Agnes, though? Dared she believe the whispered words came from her mother?

No, a cruel trick conjured by Harrow, a mirage to splinter what little sanity remained. *Why would Mother come now?* "Another conjured nightmare, no doubt!" Mabel cried to the illusion. "Do your worst, Harrow! You'll never break me, bastard!"

The wraith approached unfazed, radiating tender warmth. "It's truly me, Mabel. You have suffered such horrors, but hope still remains."

Mabel searched the gentle eyes, aching to embrace this phantom but what of trust? This had to be a trick.

"Hope?" Mabel stabbed. "You speak of hope now, in this hellhole where John was ripped from me? Where my one and only child has been stolen away and kept from me in every way except for his cries, which, might I add, has been a torment to my very soul?"

Mabel continued, "I watched them execute my innocent husband–for trying to protect me, for protecting our son! Then they ripped Thomas from my arms as I screamed and begged, condemning me to this pit. Does that sound like there's any hope left, Mother?"

Mabel waited for an answer.

Agnes said nothing.

"You remained silent, Mother! Abandoning me to this fate. And now you speak of hope?" Mabel screamed, her voice echoed through the dungeon halls. Laughter of the Accursed boomeranged back.

Agnes wore a mask of sorrow. "If only I could have prevented this cruelty, spared you such pain. But you still have the power to rise above. And rise above you must, my love."

Those tender words pierced Mabel's armour of rage and distrust.

With a broken sob, she fell into her mother's arms. "I'm lost, Mother. They've taken everything. Without John, without Thomas..." she clung to Agnes like a frightened child. She wept. She shivered. Tears streamed down her dirty cheeks.

"My dear Mabel," Agnes soothed, gently stroking her. "Though all seems lost, your story does not end here. You have such strength within, my love. I am so proud of you."

Mabel looked up with bloodshot eyes, starved for those words. Doubt lingered.

"Mabel, you must understand that your family line is one of healers, not a curse. The people of Alderwood fear and suffer from misguided righteousness, but what you have is a gift."

"A gift?!" Pulling away, Mabel's face turned to furious disbelief. The force of her reaction took Agnes by surprise, almost knocking her off balance. Mabel's hollow laugh echoed in the stony confines of the dungeon. "You dare call this a gift?" She gestured to the dark, oppressive room, her voice rising. "Can you not hear Thomas's cries echo here? It is a curse, Mother!"

Agnes's expression tightened, desperation filtering into her previously composed features. She reached out a gentle hand. "You can overcome this, Mabel. You have the power to heal, to rise again and reclaim what's rightfully yours. This is your Awakening."

Mabel violently recoiled, shaking her head. Her eyes glittered with tears. "There is no healing here, no Awakening, only death. Every breath is a bitter reminder of the life that was stolen from me, the family that I've lost!"

She collapsed to her knees in tears. "Because of you!" she cried out. If not for their shared cursed lineage, her beloved John would still draw breath, and her precious Thomas would be safe in her arms. They would be a family, simple townsfolk, living quietly with no connection to witchcraft or magic of any sort.

As Agnes began fading, Mabel clutched desperatcly at her robe. "Mother, don't leave me here alone!"

Agnes offered a sad, tender smile as she dissolved into mist. "You have the strength within you, my daughter," her voice only an echo. "Remember where you came from…"

"No, please!" Mabel begged, grasping at the fading apparition. Her fingers sliced air as Agnes vanished, leaving Mabel alone again in her cell.

She collapsed against the wall, sharp edges from the stones cut into her back. Great heaving sobs wracked her thin frame as hopelessness cloaked her.

Agnes spoke of power hidden in Mabel's blood, but what use was magic in this dungeon? It hadn't saved John from the *Seven Stones*, or Thomas from the merciless reckoning of Harrow.

"Lies...it was all lies!" Mabel cried out, her voice raw and broken. She dug her fingernails into her palms until they drew her supposed witchblood, welcoming the physical pain to distract from the anguish tearing her soul apart.

How could she tap into such a gift in this foul place? She didn't even know how to answer the most important question at that moment.

"You lied, Mother!" she screamed, clawing at her own chest for the alleged power. "I have no gift, no magic! You abandoned me to this fate!"

She slammed her fists against the wall until her knuckles split open and bled. She was used to it by now and felt no pain, only a constant numbness.

She fought only for her son. All of this was for him, her last living saviour.

She closed her eyes, steadying her breathing. She had to believe she could discover the power within. But the more she grasped for it, the more it eluded her, it was like trying to catch smoke between her fingers.

Was Thomas alive, as Agnes claimed? Or had Harrow's demons already slaughtered her precious boy? Was her boy with Harrow now, being raised by him, and what was worse... thinking... Thomas would never know his mother... thinking... she abandoned him... thinking... brain washed by Harrow and the lies of Alderwood about her... thinking... Mabel, the Witch of Alderwood... thinking... thinking... thinking... Not knowing was an agony all on its own, each possibility equally terrifying. She released a broken sob, collapsing once more to the cold stone floor.

She had never felt so weak, so lost and alone.

~*~

Mabel awoke with a gasp. The faint words *"I am always with you,"* echoed from the stones around her.

Frantically scanning the cell through leaky eyes, nothing had changed.

Except... Something was different! Something had changed!

A flash of emerald through the gloom snatched her attention. There upon the floor, illuminated by a shaft of moonlight, lay an ornate amulet on a braided leather cord.

Her breath caught in her throat as she drifted closer, entranced by the jewellery's allure. The large central gem was an oval of flawless emerald, its deep green depths flecked with azure, beckoning her to look deeper. Intricate knots and swirls of tarnished silver surrounded the stone, marked with strange arcane symbols speaking of ancient secrets.

With trembling fingers, she lifted the talisman. The amulet felt pleasantly cool and heavy in her palm, thrumming with powerful magic. Tracing the winding grooves of silverwork, she fancied each intricate knot had been carved over countless hours by timeless hands. It was real, not a trick of the mind.

Mabel closed her eyes and focused inward, searching for the healing gift within which Mother Agnes had spoken. But no matter how intensely she concentrated, nothing happened. The cold dungeon remained bleak around her.

She began pacing, weaker than she had been months before. She caressed the talisman, "Please, help me find the magic inside. Mother said I have this power! But where is it? How do I bring it forth? What must I do? Gaia, please show me the way. I beg of you!"

Only silence answered her mad hysteria. Somewhere within the dark corridors, she again heard the faint echoes of Thomas's cries. But after months trapped here, she knew it was likely another cruel illusion. So it didn't matter.

Her cries echoed through the dungeon's vast emptiness. "You lied, Mother! I have no gift, no magic!" she hurled the talisman with all her strength. It ricocheted off the iron door in a burst of sparks before clattering to the floor.

Collapsing to her knees, great heaving sobs convulsed Mabel's weakened, emaciated frame. She gazed around the cell. Harrow sought to grind her spirit to dust, extinguishing her soul's last ember of hope. Soon death would claim her here, without ever saving Thomas from the Constable. She would perish alone in this abyss, forever forgotten, doomed to become one of the Accursed Origins.

Mabel's hysteria echoed through the corridors. The ghostly wails of tormented souls mocked her feeble screams. She buried her face in her hands, weeping. Then hearing a faint skitter, she lifted her head. It was the talisman slowly dragging itself across the floor toward her. It seemed drawn to her, as if compelled by an unseen force. Mabel watched as it crept steadily closer.

Wiping away her tears with a sleeve, she lifted the talisman. Tracing the silver scrollwork surrounding the oval stone, she whispered hoarsely, "Forgive my doubt, Mother." Though her faith had wavered, she knew she must believe as Agnes did–for Thomas's sake.

She stood and slipped the cord over her head, the cool emerald settling heavily against her breast. Closing her eyes, she sought to slow her ragged breathing to calm her mind and body. She focused inward, searching for that quiet inner strength Mother Agnes insisted she possessed.

Clearing her thoughts, she focused on the talisman's energy against her skin. She imagined its power awakening her gift, flowing through her veins to heal and restore. The stone began to glow from within, bathing her in its radiance, infusing light into her weary bones.

Mabel concentrated with all her might, willing the talisman's power to awaken her own magic. But no matter

64

how intensely she focused, the cold dungeon remained unchanged around her. Frustration and doubt crept back in as the talisman's glow went away again.

She paced the cell, caressing her amulet and begging it to unlock her power. "Please, you must show me the way," but as quickly as it came, the light dimmed. Suddenly, Mabel's left foot caught on an uneven crack in the floor, twisting her ankle sharply as she fell. She heard the sickening snap of bone before her body slammed against the cold, unforgiving stones.

White-hot agony exploded through her leg as she lay crumpled and helpless. A blood-curdling scream tore from her throat, echoing off the walls. She stared down in horror at her mangled limb, bent at an impossible angle. The pain was all-consuming, unlike anything she had ever experienced before.

Her vision swam as shock and trauma threatened to drag her into unconsciousness. She fought against the black flood creeping into her mind, clawing desperately to remain awake.

Through the dizzying haze of pain, the talisman blazed against her chest, pulsating like a heartbeat. The amulet grew hot against her skin as healing magic flowed into her mutilated limb. She cried out as blistering heat radiated from the pendant into her shattered ankle, mending splintered bone and torn flesh. She watched in awe as the swelling rapidly subsided and the jagged edges of the break fused back together under the emerald glow. The pain in her leg faded to a dull ache as strength returned. Its power had healed her injury completely.

Mabel collapsed, back to the cold stone wall, spent but renewed. Gazing in disbelief at her perfectly mended limb, she burst out laughing–an incredulous, delirious, tearful spastic laugh of victory mixed with relief.

The talisman's glow diminished after unlocking its power to heal her broken form. Though she still did not fully grasp the depths of her own gift, hope blossomed anew in her weary heart. She would survive this hell, reclaim her precious child, and exact justice against those who had wronged them so cruelly, especially Constable Harrow.

She felt a renewed sense of resolve. She vowed to focus her mind and strengthen her body, preparing for the day she could fight back against her captors, the prison guards and especially Harrow. Each day trapped here would only fuel her determination to be reunited with Thomas and avenge her husband's death. She caressed the talisman at her breast, drawing courage from it. For Thomas's sake, she would never stop fighting.

As Mabel lifted the pendant to admire its beauty, her thumb traced over the emerald stone. For an instant, she thought she saw an enormous eye within the stone's depths, blinking back at her. She froze, transfixed by the massive reptilian pupil rimmed in azure flame that stared directly into her soul. It gazed at her with wisdom and curiosity, as if awakening from a long slumber. But in a blink, the eye vanished, leaving her to wonder if it had been a trick of the mystical light.

For the first time since her imprisonment, she felt the spirit of Mother Agnes, the Enchantress of Alderwood, flowing inside her.

My dear daughter, wake up! Mabel... wake... up... please wake up...

Mother? Mother! Am I awake now, Mother?

Mabel awoke screaming again, endless nightmares clung to her mind like cobwebs. She reached for the pebble to add another faint white tick to the countless marks etched into the wall.

How many months had she been trapped in this tomb now, struggling to cling to shreds of hope and sanity? She had lost count of the days long ago.

Her fingers clutched at her throat in momentary panic. The familiar cool weight of the talisman, its woven cord cutting into her skin, greeted her fingers. She traced the emerald stone compulsively, terrified it would somehow vanish if she let it go.

She caressed the stone's contours, remembering the night it had mysteriously come into her possession, and later, a reptilian eye had emerged. *What was that? Who was that?*

She glanced over at one tally encircled deeply–she had etched that mark the morning after Mother Agnes had visited her.

I am always with you…

Remembering how she frantically scanned her cell, with hopes of her mother still being there, instead a flash of emerald had snatched her attention. An ornate amulet lay upon the floor in a white pool of moonlight.

Entranced, she had drifted closer, lifting the talisman with trembling fingers. Its pleasantly cool weight and intricate silver scrollwork surrounding the emerald stone–carved by timeless hands. A gift from Mother Agnes.

"Forgive my doubt, Mother," Mabel had apologised, although her mother was why she'd been imprisoned in the first place, and she had every right to feel betrayed after all she'd been through. Worry not, though. A spark of hope penetrated the abyss just the same. Though still a prisoner, no longer did she face the shadows alone, and that was more than enough to be thankful for. Now she had a fighting chance to save her dear sweet babe.

In the weeks since, Mabel etched mark after mark into the stone wall alternating between acceptance and denial. She remembered clearly the first time the talisman's power stirred. Searing pain had exploded through her leg as it shattered, but then brilliant light had enveloped her broken bone and put it back together again.

That act had awakened her own gift. Though the talisman's magic had remained veiled ever since, it continued shielding Mabel in her most dire moments of need. And what of that enormous reptilian eye blinking back at her from the depths? She had frozen, transfixed by the slit pupil surrounded in azure flame, staring into her soul. It had gazed with wisdom and curiosity, as if awakening from a slumber. But in a blink, the eye vanished, leaving Mabel having wondered if it was real or a vision.

Chapter One: The Cry Heard Around Alderwood

What was that mystical entity dwelling within the emerald depths? Did it give the talisman its power? Her mind raced with disturbing questions she could not answer. Yet despite its mysteries, the talisman's presence comforted her. Its energy offered a sense of safety she had not felt since the day she was forced out of John's arms.

She longed to look upon the great eye again one day, to fully unravel the mysteries veiled within Mother's gift. She hoped the time would come when the entity would see fit to manifest before her. Until then, she would honour its choices, trusting it to appear when she needed it most, as it had done to heal her shattered leg when all was lost. Perhaps then she could give proper thanks.

On the wall, Mabel traced her fingers over the carved circle–approximately thirty additional tally marks earlier, though many blurred together in a haze of misery–while refusing to let go of the desperate joy sparked by the talisman's arrival roughly a month earlier.

Closing her eyes, she pressed the cool gemstone to her cracked lips, drawing what little strength she could from its energy. Amidst the shifting shadows, this relic from Mother was real, and she had to now accept her Awakening or risk losing her babe forever. She clung to it now like driftwood amidst a raging sea.

Chapter One: The Cry Heard Around Alderwood

A loud cry suddenly echoed through the maze outside her cell, closer this time, the closest he's been in months. "Thomas!" she gasped, bolting up from the foul, soggy straw. Her babe's wail–closer than ever before. Was it real this time, or just another cruel trick?

As she scanned the room, the talisman flared. Her eyes landed on the cell door–it stood ajar, rusted hinges bent outward by some unknown force. Had the talisman's power done this? The cries echoed through the open passageway. Stunned but emboldened by this chance for escape, Mabel crept towards the door, no longer caring if this was a trap.

She had no choice—she had to pursue any chance to find Thomas. Scrambling to the door, she peered out cautiously into the passageway. The dim corridor stretched onward, a welcome escape from the void of her cell. Thomas' cry echoed again, spurring her desperation. Mabel threw her bony shoulder against the door. It creaked open wider as she shoved with all her strength, tears of effort streaming down her face.

Freedom beckoned, but Mabel hesitated. Her eyes stung at the sight of the passage. Frigid air clawed at her throat. She stood at the precipice between her lifeless cell and the inescapable dungeon maze beyond.

Chapter One: The Cry Heard Around Alderwood

She whispered a prayer of gratitude as she tightened her grip on the talisman, its energy her only shield against the horrors ahead.

The rough stones underfoot oozed foul moisture, slick and treacherous. Claws skittered in the distance, echoing off the maze of winding tunnels.

The dungeon sounds were her only company.

The talisman's emerald light illuminated her way. She traced her hands along the dripping walls, edging toward freedom. Dread lay heavy in her gut. This labyrinth contained only death and pain.

Ahead, a glint of silver—a dagger mysteriously left in her path. Lifting the blade, desperation and hope warred within her. Its polished hilt bore the crest of Alderwood's Warden. An impossible stroke of luck, but she would use anything to save Thomas.

The mystic blade in hand, talisman at her breast, Mabel delved deeper as the darkness closed behind her.

Harrow was about to face the fury of her Awakening–but first, she had to find her son.

3: False Freedom

Mabel moved silently through the dreary dungeon corridors. She had long grown accustomed to navigating the filth and decay pervading this abyss after nearly a year trapped as Harrow's prisoner. Her bare feet instinctively avoided the pockets of stagnant murk that pooled across the uneven floor, having learned to numb herself, just like she had to do with the impossible smell of rot. The cracks between the stones crawled with vermin that skittered away from her cautious steps. She was used to it all now.

The emerald talisman lay cool against Mabel's breast, keeping one hand wrapped around it, as she tiptoed through the dungeon. In her other hand she clutched the Warden's Dagger, though she knew it provided only an illusion of safety. She had to ignore the invisible horrors.

She quickened her pace as Thomas's cries echoed from somewhere ahead. They resonated so close now, yet still so far away. Barred windows lined the ceiling, occasional shafts of moonlight spearing the floor from above. Mabel navigated by touch along the maze's contours, refusing to lose herself within this labyrinth. Thomas's cries were her lifeline, growing nearer with every turn.

So close now.

She moved swiftly through the passages, focused intently on locating the source of Thomas's cries. She strained her ears at each turn, desperate to discern which way his wailing echoed from. Ignoring the cold slimy stones underfoot, she pressed on, invoking a prayer to Mother Agnes under her breath. Visions of her babe alone and afraid in the dark cell for almost a year propelled her forward. She had to find him before the guard discovered her escape.

The talisman flared with light as she approached an intersection, confirming Thomas must be down the left passage. Gripping it tighter, she plunged into the darkness. The echoes grew louder, then faded, toying with her senses. She refused to lose hope. "Mama's coming, my sweet boy," she whispered. "Hold on just a little longer."

Echoing footsteps preceded the flickering torchlight as a hulking prison guard approached on inspection rounds, unaware of Mabel's escape. She shrank into a broken alcove, holding her breath waiting for him to pass. As the guard drew near, the talisman's light dimmed, cloaking Mabel in darkness as the torchlight stretched monstrous shadows across the passage walls. She tensed, scarcely daring an exhale as the guard's hulking figure lumbered by, each footfall echoing like the tolling of a grave. If he discovered her missing from her cell, escape would be impossible. She pressed deeper into the alcove, praying the blackness would hide her. The slightest sound, the barest movement, would betray her presence. Finally the guard's footsteps faded into the distance, and the talisman's light returned, helping to guide her way once more.

This sprawling labyrinth of twisting corridors and dead-ends seemed designed specifically to erode the sanity of any lost soul condemned to wander its unending passages. Yet with Thomas's muffled cries drawing closer, Mabel pressed onward, rounding another bend. She focused only on escaping with her child, guided by the talisman's light. Somewhere ahead, just around the next left bend, his frightened screams echoed again. She was getting closer. It was a miracle they had survived this long.

Turning a right corner, Mabel froze. The passage terminated abruptly in a solid stone wall marked with pulsing crimson runes that writhed in the torch flames. Half-embedded in the wall was a humanoid figure, its limbs twisted at unnatural angles. Mabel crept closer on trembling legs as icy horror clawed up her throat. Though obscured in shadow, the contorted face leering back at her from a body fused with stone was horribly, sickeningly familiar.

"John!" Tears blurred her vision, memories flooded her mind, and she dropped to her knees. She saw John's handsome face twisted in rage on the executioner's platform. Heavy iron shackles weighed down his limbs as the first 100-pound stone was hoisted above his back, poised to crush the life from his body. Mabel scrambled through the crowd as Harrow released his grip. The stone smashed down with a sickening crunch, driving the air from John's lungs in an agonised scream. Yet his eyes found Mabel's across the sea of hateful faces, silently begging her forgiveness as the next stone was raised.

As the memory receeded, Mabel grasped the talisman, desperately willing its power to save John from the wall in his Accursed state, but the magic within remained dormant.

She tore her gaze away from the horror, only for her eyes to land on the adjacent cell barely visible in the gloom. Behind it, Thomas's muffled screams were louder than ever.

Mabel choked back sobs, crawling closer to John's tortured shell fused into the stones. This was no illusion or trick. Harrow had taken John's punishment to the next level. She pressed her forehead to the wall, reaching for

John's exposed fingers where they protruded from the stone. His bone-white fingers twitched and tightened around her own with a terrified squeeze.

"John, I'm so sorry," she wept, grief and guilt threatening to crush her. "I should have saved you..." She longed to free him from this eternal agony, but knew it was impossible. Their only hope was escaping Alderwood so Thomas would not share his fate. John's sunken eyes reflected the painful understanding. She kissed his frigid fingertips, swearing she would return to end his suffering. But right now, their son needed her more.

She reluctantly tore her gaze from John's agonised face and moved to the cell on shaky legs. She slid the dagger's blade into the crack between the door and frame. The iron lock grated and stuck fast. Bracing herself, she threw her shoulder against the dagger's hilt, hearing the mechanism screech in protest. The jagged iron sliced her palm as she struggled to pry it loose. Blood dripped down her wrist but she barely felt the pain, focusing only on getting to her child.

With a final wrench, the lock broke free. Concealing the dagger, so as not to frighten Thomas, Mabel pulled open the heavy door, the rusty hinges scraping louder in the silence. She froze and listened intently, searching for any sign of the guards. The only sound was her racing heartbeat echoing in her mind.

Ripping some fabric from her tattered dress, she quickly tied it around her hand to staunch the bleeding and stepped across the threshold.

Chains hung empty from the walls. The stone floor was strewn with mouldy straw and soiled rags. She had honestly doubted that Thomas would actually be here–after so long being imprisoned, she thought her mind was playing cruel tricks, torturing her with phantom cries. Yet as her eyes adjusted, she saw a small mound stir in the corner.

Drawing closer, she made out a tiny figure shifting in the straw. Mabel's breath caught at the sight of the baby's soft curls in moonlight.

"Thomas…" she whispered.

Her frightened babe wailed at the harsh rasp of her voice. She kneeled beside him, reaching out with a careful hand.

"Hush now, you're safe," she crooned. The cries quieted at her soothing tone. The boy turned, revealing a round face smudged with dirt but otherwise healthy. Mabel gasped–after so long apart, she was finally able to gaze upon her precious babe's face once more.

Thomas studied her with a little uncertainty. Before she could move closer, his pudgy hand grabbed a chunk of bread from the floor and hurled it at her.

The hard crust struck her cheek. Instinctively she grabbed the morsel and devoured it, crumbs spilling. She had not eaten in days.

Mabel swept her son into her arms, holding him close as his giggles echoed in the cell. They had to leave. Now! Before someone heard them.

Turning back to John, Mabel moved closer, analysing the horrific fusion of flesh and stone. Thomas fussed in her arms, his chubby hand reaching toward the Accursed man as if sensing it was his father.

"No, my darling," Mabel whispered, pulling him back. She searched John's sunken eyes, begging silently for some way to free him from the Accursed.

A long moment passed with only the sound of water dripping down the walls. At last John's cracked lips moved slowly, with great effort. "Antidote..." he rasped.

Mabel stopped in her tracks. "Antidote? Is there a way to reverse this?" she asked urgently.

He gave an almost imperceptible nod before uttering a final word: "...Castle."

Her mind raced, trying to make sense of his cryptic message. Castle? Did he mean the Alderwood Castle on the outskirts of the Forest's North Region and across the Mainland? Was there truly an antidote hidden within its walls that could reverse the Accursed?

"How do you know there is an antidote in the castle, John?" Mabel asked. "Are you certain it can save you?"

Restoring his human self could be fatal. And why had her talisman remained dormant when she needed its power most to free John? It healed her. Could it not heal her beloved? The talisman felt useless against her chest.

John's sunken eyes were full of desperate hope despite her scepticism.

"I swear I will return for you," Mabel vowed, squeezing his rigid fingers. Leaving him tore her heart anew, but Thomas whimpered and squirmed in her arms, drawing her focus. She had to get their son to safety first, then solve the mystery of the antidote.

Mabel slipped back into the maze with her son. She clenched her teeth against the burning ache in her muscles. Starvation sapped her strength, but she could not fail now.

Up ahead, heavy footfalls thundered against the stones, accompanied by guttural shouts. The guards had discovered her escape. Mabel fled down the corridor, one hand against the wall to guide her steps, the other clutching Thomas close as she ran blindly through the dark.

Voices around the next bend sent Mabel darting into a side passage. She muffled Thomas's cry against her shoulder as two guards strode by, oblivious to her whereabouts. Creeping back out, she adjusted her son's weight. He grew heavier with every turn.

Each promising tunnel ended at a dead-end or circled back to a point already searched. She cradled Thomas closer, calming his whimpers lest he alert the guards. Time blurred as she traversed the endless maze.

At last she detected a draft of fresh air. They must be nearing the upper level and, hopefully, a way out. Mabel staggered faster despite her screaming muscles. Up ahead, a worn staircase spiralled up into a fathomless shadow.

She ascended the steps ignoring her exhaustion. Her legs threatened to buckle. Thomas squirmed as if sensing her weakening grip.

When Mabel reached the first landing, she sank to her knees with ragged breaths. Thomas wriggled free and began toddling down the corridor, cooing with delight at his newfound mobility.

"Thomas, stop!" Mabel rasped, lurching after him on rubbery legs. Each stride ignited new infernos across her starved body. Thomas evaded her clumsy grasp, his gleeful giggles rebounding down the passage.

Then he froze, giggles seized. Around the next bend shuffled a stooped figure draped in filthy robes, muttering words that were intangible to any that might be listening. Mabel reacted on instinct, scooping up Thomas and darting into the nearest open cell. She sank into the shadows behind the door just as the muttering drew nearer.

Through the gaps in the wood, she glimpsed Elderly Abigail dragging a laden sack. Mabel tensed in shock at the sight of the old crone who had once been a friend. Had Abigail been the one caring for Thomas all this time? The woman shuffled past, still quietly muttering to herself. Waiting until she faded from view, Mabel slipped back into the corridor.

The stairs continued upwards in disorienting spirals. Mabel focused only on climbing to the next landing, trying to ignore Thomas's cries of protest that echoed in the confined space. Moonlight speared through a barred door on the landing. That tantalising white glow drew Mabel like a moth to flame. She jammed the dagger into the lock, the last of her strength fueled by desperation. The rusted mechanism crunched and screeched before popping open.

She emerged under pale moonlight atop the parapet wall, searching for a way to the courtyard below. Nothing. She had to go back the way she came.

She descended the steps, then froze halfway down. Abigail stood waiting on the first landing, eyes wild. "The boy belongs to Constable Harrow now," the old woman rasped. "You cannot take him, witch!"

Mabel stepped back, clutching Thomas tighter. "He is mine!" she shouted.

As Abigail lunged, Mabel twisted away, shielding Thomas with her body so he would not be harmed. Abigail grabbed Mabel's wrist, dragging them both down the steep stairs in a tangle of limbs. Mabel curled herself around Thomas, taking the brunt of the impact as they tumbled into darkness.

The talisman flashed bright green, sensing her peril. It faded dull again as she staggered to her feet, ensuring her son was unharmed in the fall.

Abigail rose as well, screaming, "The witch has the boy! The witch has him!"

Mabel raised the dagger, silencing Abigail's screams. She turned to Thomas, burying his face in her chest. "Close your eyes, my love," she whispered, though after the horrors of the last year, it was too late to shield him now.

As Abigail tried to grasp for them again, Mabel pressed the blade to her throat harder and crouched down–this time nicking her skin, staring into the old woman's wild eyes, nose to nose, as blood dripped from the blade.

"You were right about me all along," Mabel spat. "Alderwood is right to hate me for what I am."

Abigail hesitated, confusion and regret warring in her expression as she gazed upon the innocent babe.

Mabel saw the change in Abigail's eyes. "Please," she implored, "let us pass. I will spare your life if you just let us leave."

Abigail's face hardened. "The boy belongs to Harrow now. You'll not leave with the heir of Alderwood, witch," she hissed.

Mabel embraced the old woman one last time. "Then you leave me no choice," she choked out, before drawing the blade swiftly across Abigail's throat. Mabel continued holding her as life drained from her body, until finally she went still. With sadness, Mabel laid Abigail's lifeless corpse gently on the floor and left her there.

Focusing again, Mabel gathered her son and fled into the gloom, the image of Abigail's death etched in her mind. She had done what was necessary to protect her son, but took no joy from it.

Mabel limped on until she came across a weathered wooden door she had not noticed before, hidden in the shadows. Iron bands criss crossed its face–the way out at last. She smashed it open and stumbled up the few crumbling steps leading outside into the cool night air of the courtyard.

Overwhelmed by her first few breaths of fresh air she had taken in after over a year, Mabel longed to savour this hard-won moment of freedom. But there was no time to waste. Adjusting her hold on Thomas, she sprinted for the open gates across the moonlit courtyard.

Freedom lay just steps ahead. Suddenly, Mabel heard heavy boots echoing from the alley beyond, freezing her in her tracks. She clutched Thomas tighter as a hulking silhouette materialised from the darkness.

Constable Harrow ducked through the gateway, his face twisted into a gruesome grin. Torches flared around him, casting his monstrous shadow over Mabel and Thomas. Though unarmed, the sheer size and power of the man radiated threat. His bloodshot eyes fixed on the baby in Mabel's arms.

"Going somewhere, witch?" his voice boomed through the courtyard.

Mabel edged back slowly, feeling like a cornered animal. Thomas stared at the looming figure and said "Da–"

"No!" she screamed.

"–Give me back my son, Mabel," Harrow rumbled, approaching with thundering footsteps.

She retreated until her back met cold stone. She had barely escaped that wretched dungeon only to be trapped again at the mercy of this demon. Holding Thomas close, she summoned the last of her strength.

"He will never be yours," she spat through trembling lips.

Harrow's grin spread wider, anticipation glinting in his eyes. "We shall see about that."

Harrow lunged with startling speed, massive hands grasping for Thomas. Mabel twisted away, shielding her son with her body. She darted towards the open gates, but

Harrow moved to block her, forcing her back against the courtyard wall.

"Give him to me!" Harrow roared.

"Stay away from us!" she clutched Thomas tighter as Harrow stalked closer. Out of the corner of her eye, she saw prison guards emerging to encircle them.

"It's over, witch," Harrow challenged.

The talisman flared with light, sensing her peril. Harrow's eyes widened in shock at the sight of her talisman. "Where did you get that?" he demanded.

He charged, arms outstretched. Mabel wasn't sure if he was reaching for her, the talisman or Thomas, all she knew was that she had to get away. Holding tightly to Thomas, she dropped and rolled, Harrow's fists slamming the stone where she had stood. Scrambling to her feet, Mabel fled along the wall, but a guard stepped into her path. She slashed with the dagger, forcing him back.

All around the courtyard, guards closed in. Harrow bellowed orders and three men rushed her at once. Feeling the strength from the talisman flow through her, she kicked hard, hearing the crack of ribs under her bare foot. She elbowed another man, whirling as the third grabbed for Thomas.

In desperation, Mabel pretended to trip, rolling clumsily with Thomas in her arms. As the guard reached for them, she kicked upwards, driving her heel brutally into his crotch. The man shrieked and doubled over, impaling himself on her dagger.

The guards hesitated, wary of Mabel's ferocity, thanks to the combination of the talisman and the years of practice with John perfecting her technique.

A raven plummeted from the night sky, white eyes gleaming. The raven's sudden appearance sparked a memory of the night Agnes had come to Mabel, its white eyes marking it as her mother's Familiar. From its claws, it dropped a bundle at her feet, a case containing her longbow and arrows.

Muscle memory took over as she swiftly nocked an arrow and let it fly into Harrow's shoulder. He staggered back with a bellow, the arrow jutting from his shoulder.

Seizing the chance, she ripped the iron ring of keys from his belt and sprinted for the courtyard gates. Behind her, his enraged roars echoed through the courtyard. "Stop her! Don't let them escape!"

Even as she fumbled with the lock, shouts arose from the darkened streets beyond the wall. Villagers streamed toward the jail, alerted by the sounds of fighting.

Torches bobbed through the gloom, revealing the mob's hateful faces twisted in anticipation.

The lock finally clicked open. As Mabel pulled the creaking gates, the mob surged forward, bloodthirsty and grasping for her.

"There's the Witch of Alderwood!" they chanted. "Seize her! Kill the witch!"

Just before the mob reached her, the talisman flared again. The burst of light blinded the villagers, causing them to recoil and shield their eyes.

Mabel slipped through the gates and plunged into the streets with her son.

The familiar village streets had become a terrifying maze with danger lurking around every corner. She fled through the alleys, the mob close on her heels. She careened around corners, slipping through narrow passages, the dagger flashing as she carved a path through anyone standing in her way. Still they pursued her, relentless and bloodthirsty.

Somewhere behind her, Constable Harrow's enraged bellow echoed through the streets. "Get the witch! Bring me my child!"

Mabel's lungs burned. Her legs could barely sustain the frantic pace as she sprinted through the village streets.

Torchlight flooded the alley behind her, revealing the mob closer on her heels. The talisman glowed as she neared a crooked wooden door halfway down the alley. Finding this escape route gave her a flicker of hope. She raced for the door, slipping on the muddy cobblestones.

Reaching the entrance, she wrenched it open and ducked inside. The room beyond was pitch black, but it was better than being torn apart by the crazed mob. She kicked the door shut and jammed her dagger through the iron handle, barricading it closed.

Seconds later, the mob reached the door. They pounded angrily on the wood, trying to break through. The door held fast, and the crowd soon moved on thinking that they had heard her footsteps down the alleyway.

Inside her dark refuge, Mabel slumped against the door, struggling to muffle her ragged breaths as the villagers' enraged cries faded. As her eyes adjusted, she saw stacks of dusty old furniture and other odds and ends–it appeared to be a storage room of some kind. It was a perfect place to catch her breath and regroup before continuing her escape from Alderwood.

She set Thomas down gently on a moth-eaten blanket and quickly tried washing herself using rainwater from a rusted barrel. The water was brackish but felt soothing on her skin.

Rummaging through the items, she found a faded dress of roughspun wool and a tattered cloak lined with rabbit fur. She shook out the garments, wafting dust into the musty air, before pulling them on. Though worn, they provided blessed warmth and modesty.

In the corner lay a forgotten leather satchel, cracked with age but still perfect for carrying useful items she could find around this place.

With care, she placed the dagger inside. Beside the satchel, she gently laid the longbow and remaining arrows into their case just as they had arrived bundled together, minus three arrows from her fight with Constable Harrow.

She sank down beside Thomas, prepared to wait out the night if need be. She replenished herself with stale bread and dried meat from the pantry.

As she ate, Mabel studied her son. He had grown so much, no longer the tiny babe she last cradled over a year ago. His round cheeks showed he had been well cared for in her absence. Her heart swelled with love and relief to have him back safely in her arms.

"Oh Thomas, my sweet boy," she whispered, stroking his hair as he gazed up with wide hazel eyes. He babbled cheerful sounds, music to her ears after the disjointed echoes of his cries resonated through the dungeon for endless nights. She had feared she might never see him laugh again.

Yet now Thomas smiled up at her, his small warm hands unfazed by her haggard appearance as he patted at her cheek. "Mama's here now, my sweet," Mabel murmured through joyful tears. "I'll never leave you again."

The tender moment faded as he began to fuss and cry, his cheeks reddening with exertion. She instinctively held him close, rocking to soothe his fitful wails. She sang an old lullaby Abigail had sung to her a long time ago, the familiar words now imbued with new meaning:

"Hush now, my dear one,
there's nothing to fear,
mama will keep you safe,
always near,
Gaia watches over with love,
so sleep now, my child, guarded from above."

At the soothing rhythm of her voice, his eyes drifted shut. As his tears subsided, she kept singing until his chest rose and fell in a peaceful sleep.

She studied his innocent face–those thick lashes resting on round cheeks flushed from crying, his pink lips parted slightly in slumber. Gratitude swelled within, for Abigail's care, though Mabel knew not what darkness had twisted the woman in the end.

She held Thomas close as he slept, savouring his comforting weight in her arms. She remembered the endless nights in her dungeon cell, hearing only his cries. Now they were together again, having survived that unending hell. Dawn would soon break, bringing with it hope of escape and a new life beyond these cursed walls.

After securing the room, she settled on the dusty floor beside Thomas, dagger in hand. She kept watch through the long night, her mind turned again to Timothy Harrow—the constable's son who had so viciously condemned her—who had hissed the unspoken name of "Agnes..." It felt like a century ago. She had puzzled over it many times before while rotting in her cell, never coming any closer to answers.

Did someone betray her trust and reveal the truth? She thought no one but Aiden and John knew about Mother Agnes. Witchcraft was forbidden in Alderwood.

Mabel shuddered. She had taken pains to blend into Alderwood unnoticed. How had Timothy discovered her mother's true nature? Perhaps he had overheard a conversation or maybe...

Had Timothy harnessed wicked magic through the dark arts in the Alderwood Forest to pierce the shadows surrounding her lineage? There was much about Timothy Harrow that Mabel still did not know.

She remembered the terror of seeing him late one night, his ghoulish Accursed face peering through the barred ceiling window. His skin was deathly pale and mottled, practically rotting off the bone in places. The hungry eyes that bore into her were no longer the boyish blue of Timothy Harrow, but instead glowed with unnatural fire. Foetid drool dripped from snarled lips to reveal a projection of broken teeth ready to rend flesh from bone before he turned away and stalked back into the night.

Mabel stroked Thomas' curls as he slept beside her. She allowed her mind to envision the life awaiting them beyond Alderwood's cursed borders. No more languishing in a lightless dungeon, with only faint echoes of Thomas' cries through the corridors. She dreamed of a cottage nestled in a vibrant valley, the garden overflowing with flowers. Thomas would play freely, unburdened by the mysterious Origins of Alderwood. At night, John would return from his labours as a stonemason, embracing his family after their separation. As a skilled craftsman, John would have honourable work constructing buildings and monuments. They would sit by the crackling fire, their hearts overflowing with light after so many days in Alderwood's darkness.

More trials lay ahead before that dream could become reality. John had hinted of an antidote in Alderwood Castle that could break his Accursed hell. Mabel knew little of this supposed cure, yet had to trust John's certainty. No one fully understood the Accursed–it was said they arose amidst the Black Death, when the Avonars, a secretive cult of dark magic practitioners, conducted experiments trying to reverse the plague. However, their sinister rituals instead transformed the dead into unnatural monsters that Alderwood knew as the Accursed today.

As the first rays of dawn crept into the musty room, Mabel steeled her resolve. She remained sceptical that such a cure existed, yet had to try for John's sake. It was the only chance she had to free him. She would fight through Alderwood's darkness to save John, no matter the cost. Only then could they find a new life beyond this accursed place and be a family again.

~*~

Mabel had finally opened her eyes for the last time in the village of Alderwood. Rays of sunlight streamed through cracks in the crumbling stone walls. It was time to gather Thomas and their sparse belongings and leave this place.

As Mabel wrapped Thomas in the moth-eaten blanket to conceal his identity, he fussed and whimpered. She hushed his cries, whispering "Shhh, my darling, just a little longer." The baby continued squirming in her arms. Her heart hammered—one scream could doom them. It was a miracle he had been so quiet through the night. Now she prayed his cries would remain muffled just a little longer as she prepared to make their escape.

Suddenly, a foul smell arose. Thomas had soiled himself. Mabel stifled a frustrated sigh. She had nothing clean for him to wear. Leaving the filthy rags on him would draw unwanted attention.

Having no other clothes for him, she had no choice but to do her best. She used strips of fabric torn from the blanket to clean and wrap Thomas. She then pulled her own cloak low over her gaunt face before lifting her freshly wrapped but still fussing baby. "I know my love, but we must be brave," she whispered through his muffled cries. With Thomas secured tightly to her breast, Mabel slipped out the door.

Outside, wisps of chimney smoke curled into a pastel dawn sky. The chill air carried scents of baking bread, smoked meats, and damp earth. Villagers were beginning to stir, but the streets remained mostly empty. Quiet as shadows, Mabel glided into the sparse foot traffic, turning her face from the occasional passerby.

As they navigated through the outskirts of the village, Thomas began to whimper again. "Shhh, we're nearly there my sweet," Mabel crooned softly. Her heartbeat quickened at the sight of the fortress of ancient oaks ahead. She paused alongside a vegetable cart, pretending to inspect parsnips while soothing Thomas. "Just a little further my love."

Once through the gates, she quickened her pace, avoiding the guardsman's roaming eyes. Soon cottages gave way to farmland. The scent of tilled soil mixed with woodsmoke hung in the air. At long last, she reached the sheltering eaves of the forest, obscured by early morning mist.

She released a trembling breath, looking into the forest's shadowed depths. Mighty oak and elm branches formed an impenetrable canopy, blotting out the rising sun. The scent of damp earth and decay permeated the still air. This was not a living wood, but a primordial entity shrouded in perpetual gloom.

As she stepped deeper into the forest, she prayed the dark rumours were not true. Stories had long persisted of unnatural Origins lurking in these woods, horrors far worse than any mob. Whispers of giant wolves with blood-red eyes, shadow beings that blended into mist, ancient folklores come alive to prey on lost souls.

A fallen tree forced them into a ravine. The baby wailed but she could not stop, stumbling over slick roots as footsteps pounded the ridge above. Thorns tore her skin and cloak as she scrambled through the briars.

The true horror was what might find them first in the Alderwood Forest. The villagers wished only to burn her flesh. The things that were reported to dwell here feasted on souls, relished suffering and haunted dreams with eternal unrest. She could not shake the creeping dread that the forest's curse had only just begun to bare its fangs. As darkness stole over the woods, Mabel knew their trials had only just begun.

She hurried along the winding forest trail, clutching Thomas tightly to her chest. A chill crept down her spine as tendrils of mist coiled around them, carrying the scents of damp earth and decay. She constantly glanced back, ears straining for any sound of pursuit from Constable Harrow or the angry villagers. Her escape out of the village had been almost too easy–perhaps they wanted the Origins of the Alderwood Forest to tear her limb from limb.

There was no other way out of Alderwood. Going through the forest was the only way, and she wouldn't be followed, or so she had hoped. In truth, Constable Harrow would never let them simply slip away. He was obsessed with reclaiming Thomas at any cost. He had some crazy obsession with replacing his deceased son with hers.

4: Forest Origins

The Alderwood Forest was the most feared region in all of England, filled with horrific Origins passed down in legend. Towering ancient trees with gnarled bark and twisted branches blocked out the sun, leaving one to wander in perpetual dusk. The only light came from monstrous Origins with glowing crimson eyes and dagger-like fangs dripping blood, their misshapen forms casting a nightmarish illumination as they marched like ants through the mist. Strange cries and howls echoed through the fog, belonging to creatures not of this world ready to tear apart any lost soul. Mabel had heard tales of beasts lurking within, their talons sharp like sickles, their eyes burning like hot coals watching from the shadows. And worse things too–demons and wraiths with deathly cold breath that could freeze a man's courage, leaving him lost for eternity in the maze of trees.

No one had ever gotten close enough to the fabled pulsing portal at the forest's core and lived to tell the tale. As she ventured deeper into the woods, a swelling sense of dread knotted her stomach and her heart thundered rapidly in her chest. The mist swirled thicker now, concealing the path ahead and disorienting her senses. She pressed onward through the haze, feeling forced astray by the magic of the forest, yet she was determined to escape Alderwood and that meant going through this cursed forest.

Her first goal was to reach the Avanor's infamous Alderwood Castle on the other side, which held the potential antidote to reverse the curse and free John.

She braced herself for any of the alleged Origins that might lie ahead in waiting while adjusting her grip on Thomas.

Mabel shuddered as she recalled the torment she had already endured–the lack of food leaving her dizzy and weak, the constant thirst that burned her throat, having to live in her own filth unable to clean herself. And worst of all, hearing Thomas' screams day and night. The helplessness she felt listening to his agony was the worst trauma she had ever known. Nothing could be worse than that. Even facing the merciless Origins of the Alderwood Forest seemed a better fate.

She adjusted her grip on Thomas again, this time moving him to the left side. She had to keep moving forward, no matter what.

As they neared an unknown danger, the talisman pulsed in warning. She froze, listening intently through the fog. A clicking arose, along with the snap of monstrous jaws.

Rounding a bend, Mabel drew in a sharp breath. A massive bristly-furred spider, an unnamed-Origin, lurked just ahead, its multitude of eyes glowing crimson in the dim forest. Bright green venom dripped from foot-long fangs as its clawed legs tore apart some poor Origin-prey, granting a horrific glimpse of its true size. Mabel recoiled in terror and shoved Thomas' face into her shoulder.

Just before the giant arachnid noticed them, the talisman flared brightly. The Origin reared back with an ear-piercing screech as the light seared its many eyes. Seizing her chance, Mabel slipped away undetected into the mist.

An Alderwood Origin surfaced in Mabel's mind as she passed a pond–tales that the clear body of water was home to a vengeful spirit named Amara who dragged victims to a watery grave. She shuddered, quickening her pace around the far edge.

A blood-curdling scream pierced the misty air–Harrow's voice, though strangely distorted. She froze, holding Thomas even tighter. Through the knotted trees she glimpsed the Constable crashing recklessly toward them, face contorted in rage.

"The talisman won't save you this time!" he bellowed.

She shrank back. Though he hadn't seen her or Thomas yet, his enraged shouts sent spikes of fear through her. He had spotted the talisman during their struggle yesterday. But what did he know of its power?

Diving behind a large oak, she hid as Harrow's thunderous voice roared out closer now.

"Give me the talisman, witch, and you can keep the boy!" he cajoled. "Just hand it over!"

This offer confused Mabel. She thought Harrow wanted only Thomas, not some bauble. What did he know about her talisman? This had to be a deception–yet his words raised a tempting thought. If the talisman could buy Thomas's freedom, would she make that trade?

No, she couldn't trust the Constable to be a man of his word.

She hurried on, and abruptly the trail cnded at a murky pond. Fog curled over black water that disappeared into nothingness. Desperately she searched for a way around, but the dark pool stretched endlessly in both directions.

She was trapped–and Harrow's thunderous voice rang out behind her.

"Last chance! The talisman for the boy's life!" He sounded deranged, savage. "You can't escape me, witch! Give me the boy!"

She whirled, seeking an escape, but the skeletal trees offered no hope. What did Harrow truly want–her son or her talisman? He seemed to change his demands impossibly fast.

A beautiful melody arose unbidden through the mist, faint yet beckoning. Heart pounding, she followed the strange notes through the fog-shrouded woods in an opposing direction, unsure what other unseen Origins lay ahead. She pushed past branches and saw a shadowy wraith seated upon a moss-covered log, its fleshless fingers playing a bonepipe.

Glowing emerald eyes flared within its skull, fixing upon Mabel. Her talisman pulsed in response. She stumbled backwards, horrified yet transfixed.

Then two shouts split the silence–"The boy!" a crazed roar from one direction. "The talisman!" the same voice bellowed from another. She whirled, confused and afraid. Two Harrows? Impossible! Some evil enchantment plagued her mind.

The piper's gaze darted between the shouts before resting upon Mabel. It lifted one skeletal hand, beckoning her closer as the bonepipe trilled faster, more insistently. She backed away from the creeping doom.

Harrow's voice rang out again, closer behind her. "I'll spare you both–if you surrender the talisman."

Mabel went very still. *Spare us both? After all he had done? Nothing but lies and deception...* This place warped the mind with cruel illusions. The Harrow she knew would never show mercy.

The piper's melody drifted through the mist. Mabel's hand fastened around the talisman. She closed her eyes and said a quick prayer to Gaia to help her protect Thomas from this nightmare realm.

When she opened her eyes, both wraith and pond had vanished. Constable Harrow stood sneering before her, hand outstretched. "What's it going to be, witch? The boy or the talisman?"

Cold understanding washed over her. This was not Constable Harrow–some cunning, shape-shifter Origin had stolen his form–probing for weakness. She glared back steadily, refusing to show her fear.

Then she turned and fled into the mist, as the demon's mocking laughter pursued her. She had to get away, but how could she escape this fake Constable Harrow? Her mind reeled–this had to be one of the fear-feasting creatures birthed by the heart of Alderwood. The hellish portal was said to be guarded by demonic entities and horrors crafted by the devil himself to punish any mortal who dared draw near. Mabel had heard spine-chilling tales of previous travellers being ripped limb from limb by writhing serpents with fangs as long as daggers after getting too close.

She stumbled into a clearing and gasped—before her stood two identical ornate chests, carved from dark wood with a large letter C engraved on each. Strange arcane symbols surrounded the letter, their meanings unclear.

Behind her, the false Harrow's crazed shouts drew nearer, demanding, "Give me the talisman, witch! You cannot escape me!" while the real Constable Harrow roared with matching ferocity, "The boy is mine, Mabel! He will be raised as my heir!"

"You shall never have him, you monster!" she cried out. "Thomas is no longer your pawn, Harrow! Let us be, and we won't return to Alderwood ever again!"

Harrow's thunderous footsteps crashed through the underbrush toward her. With no time to think, she wrenched open one chest. She tucked Thomas inside, shushing his frightened whimpers, then slammed the lid shut, praying it would shield him. The chest latched shut immediately. She tried to reopen it but it was locked tight. Thomas was trapped within. Frantically she pounded the lid, clawing at the edges until her fingers bled. She screamed his name but only silence responded. The chest had swallowed him completely. Fighting back tears, she turned to face Harrow, channelling her anguish into rage.

Fury and fear flowed through her. Mabel drew her longbow and nocked an arrow, ready to end this nightmare.

Harrow burst into the clearing, startling Mabel and causing her to drop the bow, his face a mask of madness and desperation. His eyes were twin infernos, burning with unnatural hunger. He moved with predatory grace, a hunter who had finally cornered his prey.

"You have defied me for the last time, witch!" he roared. "I will gut you like a stuck pig!" He gave her a sadistic grin, but which Harrow was this in front of her?

Mabel barely had time to draw her dagger as Constable Harrow, whether real or fake, slammed into her. She screamed, stabbing wildly as they crashed to the ground, the talisman flailing around her neck with no life or will to aid her. She clawed at Harrow's face as he choked her, their eyes locked in a vicious struggle. His massive hands crushed her slender throat, black spots swimming across her dimming vision.

Summoning her last ounce of strength, she seized the fallen arrow and drove it through his left eye. He released her in pain, rocking in torment on his back.

Mabel scrambled away on her hands and knees.

"You took my boy from me!" he thundered. "Now I will take yours!"

The real Harrow ripped out the arrow, the gruesome wound not slowing him. The hulking man stalked toward her, blood streaming down his face. Then his form shimmered, slowly dissolving into the mist. She watched in horror as he evaporated before her eyes, leaving only silence.

Alone now, she sagged against a tree, gulping for air. She scanned the woods for any sign of the false Harrow, but saw only swirling fog. Just another cruel illusion.

A stillness hung over the forest. The mist muffled any sounds, pressing close with unnatural clamminess. The trees leaned in around her. But she could not rest yet. Thomas urgently needed her.

Mabel rushed to the chest, afraid of what she would find. The latches had unlocked on their own while she battled Harrow. She carefully lifted the heavy lid.

Emptiness greeted her. Thomas was gone. A fresh wave of horror washed over her.

A sob escaped her lips. She had lost her babe again, this time to the most dangerous region in all of Alderwood. He could be anywhere by now, swallowed by the Forest's magic.

"Thomas!" she cried out, her distress echoing through the mist. She had sacrificed everything, been through hell, only to fail him again in the end. All hope felt lost.

Holding on to the dagger so hard it cut into her palm joining other injuries, she stared wildly around her. Glowing eyes peered from the darkness. She had to find Thomas before the twisted Origins claimed him forever.

But where to even start in this infinite forest?

Mabel stumbled through the Forest, her breath coming in panicked gasps. The trees leered down at her like disfigured sentinels, a shroud of greenery blotting out the sky. Thomas could be anywhere in this Gaiaforsaken place–if he was even still alive. That thought sent her heart into a frenzied panic. She had to find him.

Something snapped behind her. She whirled, dagger clutched in white knuckles. Only the mist greeted her, thick and suffocating. She knew she wasn't alone. The hissing wraiths and prowling beasts of Alderwood lurked nearby, watching her. Hunting her.

Malevolent eyes flashed crimson in the gloom. Peering closer, Mabel made out the silhouette of a man emerging from the trees, his muscular frame rippling in an unnatural, bestial way. As he stepped forward, she glimpsed fangs jutting from his snarling mouth and claws tipping his fingers.

The Alderwolf's breath drew steadily closer. The air itself was electric, charged with the forest's power. It called to the witchblood in her veins. The talisman pulsed. She broke into a frantic run trying to get as far as possible away from the Alderwolf as fast as she could.

The trees waved, reaching for her with knotted, claw-like branches that tore at her dress and hair. She crashed through a tangle of briars into a bleak clearing.

A vast black lagoon stretched before her, its lifeless waters concealing unfathomable depths. It was ringed by barren trees that stooped like haggard crones, their skeletal limbs grasping outward as if to snare any who drew near.

The opaque surface rippled as a slender, wraithlike figure rose from its depths. Fiery locks fanned out around her haunting face, pale and beautiful yet cold. Her black eyes were empty pools, devoid of warmth or compassion. Full ruby lips parted to reveal needle-like fangs as the mermaid glided onto land.

"Your baby is here," the Origin intoned, her voice musical yet tinged with slight deception. From the mere came a child's cries. "Come to me, and I will take you to him..."

Mabel approached the pond's shore slowly, stones slippery underfoot. She strained to see into the thick, oily depths. "How do you know about my child?" she asked warily, not yet trusting the mermaid.

"Word travels quickly in the Alderwood Forest," the Origin replied in serene tones. "Come, let me take you to Thomas..."

Mabel waded into the pond. The talisman pulsed as if sensing danger. She ignored the warning, consumed by the need to save her son.

The water was icy and strangely viscous, clutching at her legs.

"Thomas!" Mabel cried out, moving deeper. Murky liquid swirled up to her knees. It was not water, but something archaic and alive.

The mermaid seized Mabel's ankles, talons digging into her flesh. Mabel screamed as she was jerked off balance, crashing into the water. She thrashed desperately but the Origins's hold was unbreakable as she was dragged into the mermaid's lair.

The world faded to black as she was pulled under the icy black water. She clawed and kicked but felt her strength already waning. Her ears rang and her lungs burned as the mermaid plunged her deeper. Strange images flashed through her mind–was the Origin stealing her memories?

Scraping the bottom, her hands searched frantically through the muck until, miraculously, they closed around the hilt of her dagger. It must have fallen from her satchel during the struggle. Thank Gaia, for small miracles.

Gripping it tightly and summoning the power of the talisman, she swiped upward, the blade lodging in lithic skin. A muffled shriek reverberated through the depths. Mabel pulled desperately at the hilt, trying to break the dagger free from the Origin's leathery stone-like throat.

Chapter One: The Cry Heard Around Alderwood

The mermaid burst upward, pulling Mabel's head from the water by her soaked hair. Needle-like fangs glinted in the gloom as the fiend gave a bone-chilling grin.

Mabel struggled wildly as the mermaid's fangs sank into her shoulder. She could feel the Origin ingesting her blood, invading her mind. The mermaid sorted through her memories, seeking something.

"You're the daughter of Agnes," the mermaid hissed, her grin taunting. "Your witchblood shall sustain us for eternity!" Hunger flickered in the Origin's eyes.

Mabel thrashed in the mermaid's viselike grip, the icy waters churning around her. From the shore came a distant, crazed shout–"The talisman belongs to me, witch!" The false Harrow was still pursuing her, obsessed with claiming her talisman for reasons still unknown to her.

With a feral scream, using all the strength she could summon from the talisman, Mabel ripped the dagger from the mermaid's neck, black blood oozing from the wound. The mermaid released her hold on Mable to clutch the gash. Mabel used what little strength she had left to swim back to the shore while the Origin clutched its mutilated neck, cursing her.

"Your boy will suffer for this!" the mermaid gurgled as obsidian blood spread beneath the murky surface.

Mabel collapsed on the bank, gagging up tainted water. The threat sent ice through her veins–she had to find Thomas before the mermaid found him. She feared what might happen if she failed.

The raven's piercing cry split the silence as it dove at the mermaid, sharp beak gouging its thick flesh. Mabel watched as the raven harried the fiend into the midnight depths.

Then, with no time to lose, she rose on trembling legs to follow the familiar's flight into the mist-veiled woods. But where exactly was it taking her? Mabel could only stumble after the bird, desperate for guidance in the Alderwood Forest.

"Please, lead me to my son," she pleaded. The raven remained silent, guiding her deeper through the oaks.

The false Harrow's crazed shouts rang out nearby, demanding she surrender the talisman. Her heart pounded. How had he found her trail so quickly? She pushed on desperately through the fiery pain in her legs.

"It's over, witch!" The voice seemed right behind her now, heavy with menace. "That talisman will complete my collection!"

She burst into a clearing, the raven landing on a branch above. No sign of her pursuer–had she lost him?

Then the false Harrow stalked from the trees, eyes burning greedily at the talisman around her neck. "End of the line," he growled. "That talisman is finally mine!"

He moved with startling speed, massive hands closing around her throat before she could react. She clawed wildly but his grip was unbreakable, her vision darkened.

With a sadistic grin, the false Harrow ripped the talisman away, the cord snapping as he threw Mabel across a small body of water.

Pain exploded through her skull as she hit the rocky shore.

~*~

Mabel found herself in the cosy cottage that had once been their happy home. Late morning sun streamed in through the paned glass windows, illuminating the humble room. Dried herbs hung from the timber beams, filling the air with their earthy aromas. A stew bubbled over the hearth, tendrils of fragrant steam rising from the iron pot.

Nearby in his hand-carved cradle, baby Thomas cooed and gurgled happily up at his mother. She gazed down at him, her heart swelling with joy and pride. He was swaddled in a soft linen blanket she had embroidered with wildflowers and sparrows. His tiny fists reached up toward her eagerly.

"There's my beautiful boy," she murmured, lifting him into her arms. Thomas gurgled again, nuzzling against her. She planted a tender kiss atop his head, breathing in his sweet scent.

At that moment the front door opened and John entered, back from a morning spent tending their livestock in the meadow. His face lit up when he saw Mabel and the babe.

"And how is my little family doing on this fine day?" John said brightly, embracing them both. He tickled Thomas gently under the chin, eliciting a giggle from the infant.

She smiled up at her husband, her heart full, bursting with joy. "Perfect now that you're home," she replied.

His presence always filled their cottage with warmth and laughter. He had sturdy, dependable hands that could as easily cradle Thomas as wield a hammer or scythe.

After a hearty lunch of stew and bread, he left to assist a neighbour whose cow was soon to calf. "I'll be back before supper," he promised with a parting kiss.

She spent the afternoon winding yarn from fleece and weaving on her loom, keeping one eye on Thomas as he lay swaddled in a basket nearby. She sang soothing lullabies to him, eliciting small gurgles and coos.

When John returned, they sat down to a simple but nourishing supper of roasted pheasant, leek porridge and blackberry preserves. Thomas slept soundly in Mabel's arms as she cradled him close.

Later, they bundled Thomas in soft blankets and lay beneath the stars in an open meadow, naming constellations for him.

"Look there, little one," John said softly, pointing up at the night sky. "That is Ursa Major, the Great Bear. And next to it shines Polaris, the North Star that guides lost travellers."

Thomas watched with wide eyes full of wonder, entranced by the vast beauty above. His tiny hand reached up as if trying to grasp the twinkling stars. Eventually his eyes drooped closed in slumber.

John carefully carried him back inside and laid him in his cradle. Mabel tucked the blanket snugly around him, marvelling at his tiny curled fists and sweet sleeping face. Her dear, innocent son.

Chapter One: The Cry Heard Around Alderwood

After a few moments gazing lovingly at the dozing babe, John drew Mabel into their own bed. He kissed her as they came together, reaffirming their devotion. She lay encircled in her husband's strong arms listening to his steady heart. Mabel sighed in perfect contentment. The future ahead seemed bright and full of joyous promise. This was the life in Alderwood she had always longed for.

Mabel's eyes flew open, her head throbbing, and vision blurred with waves of pain. Reaching up, she felt coarse bandages wrapped around her head. She winced as her fingers found a lump where she had struck a rock after the false Harrow had stolen her talisman.

That deceitful shapeshifting Origin manifested as its prey's deepest fears, concealing its true name and form to feed on their terror. Her greatest dread was the corrupt Constable Harrow claiming her beloved son, so the cunning Origin had taken his appearance to torment her.

As her eyes adjusted to the room, she searched her memories, trying to recall how she came to be in this unfamiliar place. The last she remembered was the false Harrow's massive hands tearing away her emerald talisman, its etched reptilian eye seeming to flare in protest as the artefact was stripped from her neck.

She had felt so exposed, so helpless without its power to merge with her witchblood. The talisman was her only defence against the dark forces of the Alderwood Forest. Without it, recovering Thomas would be impossible.

Then came the sickening crack of her head. Mabel shuddered, fingers going back up to her bandages. Someone had tended to her while she was unconscious, applying healing poultices of yarrow and comfrey to reduce inflammation before carefully wrapping her wound. They had carried her body to this shelter and treated her. But who, and where was her rescuer now?

Mabel scanned the cottage. It was sparsely furnished, humble and rudimentary. She lay on a thin straw mattress tucked in the corner, covered by a tattered wool blanket that provided little warmth. Heavy shutters blocked out any light or view of the outside world.

An iron pot hung over cold ash and embers in the fireplace, evidence of a recent fire. The room felt cold and damp. Mabel shivered. The only door looked to be barred from outside. Was she a prisoner here?

Chapter One: The Cry Heard Around Alderwood

Her body protested every movement, but she had to try standing. Holding tightly to the bedpost, she managed to rise unsteadily to her feet. The effort left her sweating and nauseated, but she swallowed against the bile rising in her throat.

Step by step, with trembling hands steadying herself against the cottage's furnishings, she explored her surroundings. A simple wooden table held a pitcher of fresh water, a loaf of hard bread, and a small knife.

She lifted the pitcher with shaking hands and gulped the cool water, spilling some down her chin in her urgency. When had she last eaten or drunk? Her memories were too fragmented to recall.

The bread, though stale, called to her empty stomach. Mabel forced herself to chew slowly, knowing she'd be ill if she bolted it down. As she ate, strength gradually returned to her limbs. She would need every bit of energy to brave the woods.

Glancing around the cottage, she spotted the leather satchel lying in the corner along with her longbow and one arrow left. At least she would not be defenceless when she ventured back into the forest.

At last she made it to the shuttered window after what felt like an eternity. She fumbled with the rusty latch before shoving it open, inhaling the damp, earthy scents of the forest. Mist coiled beyond the window, but in the distance, she could make out a dark fortress of gnarled oaks marking the edge of Alderwood Forest. Beyond the treeline, the hazy silhouette of the Mainland was just visible through the fog. Somewhere across those fields lay the small shape of the Alderwood Castle.

Leaning heavily on the window ledge, she fought back a sob. Somewhere out in the forest, Thomas, was alone and afraid. She had no idea where to start looking. She had to find him, but she could barely stand, much less search.

"Thomas!" Mabel cried out, her voice echoing unanswered. She had sacrificed everything to protect him, suffered over a year of torture from Constable Harrow, losing her husband to the Accursed, imprisoned in a dungeon cell, forced to listen as her babe's cries going unanswered, battled Accursed Origins and even lost her talisman to one of those things.

"Damn you, Harrow!" Mabel screamed, hands clenched into fists. "And damn the villagers for believing your lies! May the Accursed feast on your soul for all eternity!"

She seized the porcelain pitcher of water from the table and hurled it against the wall where it exploded. She cursed the false Harrow for not only ripping away her talisman but with it, her only chance at finding her child, "Damn you!"

Exhausted, she crumpled to her knees amidst the pieces of broken porcelain, jagged shards digging into her skin. She cared not for the pain nor the blood. Heaving tears burst from deep within as she unleashed a torrent of grief. Everything she had done to shield Thomas had been for nothing. Without the talisman's power, how would she ever find him in the Alderwood Forest now?

When her weeping finally subsided, Mabel wiped her eyes and lifted her head. She had to pull herself together and think. Wallowing in despair would not help Thomas.

She rose and shoved open all the creaking shutters for the sweet forest air, desperate for any light she could get.

Though she had reached the outskirts of the Alderwood Forest, Mabel knew she was not free yet. Not without Thomas.

Turning back, she eyed a blood-soaked heap in the corner—a corpse, the cottage's former inhabitant she assumed, which she hadn't noticed before in her fits of inconsistent hysteria. Giving it a wide radius, she backed away, eager to be gone from this place.

A harsh caw drew Mabel's attention back to the open window. Perched on the sill was the raven, a dead hare clutched in its talons. It dropped the hare on the window ledge before Mabel, a gift of sustenance she desperately needed.

Her heart swelled with hope—her mother's familiar seemed to never be too far away, and somehow always knew exactly how to help. The raven fixed its intense gaze upon her.

"Please, do you know where my son is?" she implored. She bombarded the raven with desperate queries, clutching its feathers as it cocked its head.

The raven took flight, soaring out into the mist-veiled trees. Mabel rushed to the window, scanning the gloom until the familiar vanished from sight. She whirled at the sound of an awful moan behind her.

The blood-soaked corpse lurched upright with a dreadful groan, grasping at Mabel with its rotted skeletal hands as it staggered nearer. It seized her shoulders with shocking strength, yellowed nails digging into her skin, bits of flesh sloughing off its putrid arms.

Chapter One: The Cry Heard Around Alderwood

The Accursed's jagged teeth ripped into her throat just as the thatched ceiling exploded inward. A cloaked man dropped through the hole, robes billowing around him. He wore a hood that obscured his face in shadow, and his clothing was simple and handmade. In one leather-gloved hand he gripped a sword, its razor-sharp blade glinting in the dim light.

With astonishing speed and precision, the swordsman brought the blade down in a sharp arc, slicing clean through the Accursed's neck. Dark blood sprayed across Mabel's face as the severed head fell to the floor with a sickening thud, rolling to a stop at her feet.

Mabel clasped a hand to her mangled throat as hot blood poured between her fingers. The bite had ripped away flesh, leaving a gruesome, gaping hole. Fiery pain lanced through her neck with each heartbeat. Her vision swam as scarlet dripped down her chest.

Yet she did not cry out. After enduring so much horror in Alderwood, she had learned to bear even grievous injuries with hardened composure. Survival was all that mattered now.

As the eerie glow faded from the severed head's eyes, the swordsman turned to Mabel. He lowered his hood to reveal a face weathered by care yet achingly familiar.

She recognized the swordsman instantly.

It was her father, Aiden.

"You!" she spat, rage boiling up inside her. She trembled with fury as she stood before him for the first time since his abandonment. The instant Alderwood discovered she was the daughter of the witch, he had vanished from the village that very day. Coward.

Aiden's crimson eyes narrowed, his scarred face impassive. With predatory smoothness, he approached the Accursed's corpse. Then he ripped into the putrid flesh with his teeth like a feral beast, the wet rending sounds of his feeding filling the cottage.

Revulsion shuddered through Mabel as she watched her father feast on the Accursed Origin's flesh. She knew of only one Origin capable of such an act–Alderwolves. A horrific thought crossed her mind as she watched in horror–could he be one of those beasts? Was it the same Alderwolf from before?

This was nothing like the gentle, warm-hearted man she once knew. Some dark force had transformed him into a voracious monster. She recalled a childhood filled with his loving hugs and kind smiles. Now his handsome face was cold and hard, his familiar eyes replaced by crimson pits brimming with primordial hunger.

Her mind raced, struggling to reconcile the fiend before her with the beloved father she cherished. Part of her refused to accept that the gentle man who raised her could be fully consumed by such evil. For Thomas's sake, she clung to the desperate hope that some part of Aiden's humanity yet lingered within this hellish shell of a monster.

When Aiden finally rose, he growled, "There's no time for questions," his mouth stained with dark blood. "If you wish to see Thomas again, listen closely."

Mabel contained her rage and forced herself to give a curt nod. She met his piercing gaze with venomous fury. As much as she despised him for abandoning her, Thomas needed them both now more than ever.

"Where is my babe, Father?"

"The Black Marsh," rasped Aiden.

Her eyes widened in confusion. "The Black Marsh? But how could he be there?"

She wracked her mind, trying to make sense of his words. Thomas had been in the chest. How had he vanished before her eyes?

Understanding dawned, a sickening possibility surfaced. "The chest I hid Thomas in... was it one of the Cursed Chests?"

He nodded grimmly.

Chapter One: The Cry Heard Around Alderwood

Horror choked Mabel as the implications crashed over her. By placing Thomas inside, she had unintentionally offered him up as a sacrifice. And the nearest Cursed Chest for the sacrifice to be transferred to was in the Black Marsh.

"No!" she cried. "Tell me it isn't true! We have to find him before..."

She trailed off, unable to give voice to the unthinkable outcome if they did not succeed. *Has anyone ever actually survived this curse?*

Aiden embraced her. "Pull yourself together, girl! Hysterics will not help him now."

Aiden's burning gaze bored into Mabel's. "The sun sets on the boy's life tomorrow at dusk. You must reach the Black Marsh before then."

She paused, noticing Aiden's word choice. "Aren't you coming with me?"

"I cannot," he admitted.

"It's the least you could do after abandoning me, Father!"

"I did not abandon you!" he screamed, and silence fell over the cottage. "I got bit by an Alderwolf..."

A tense silence fell between them. Mabel studied her father's face, taking in the dark blood smeared around his mouth and the soulless crimson eyes. Her suspicion was confirmed–Aiden had become an Alderwolf, Origins known to feast on the Accursed. It was rumoured that long ago, a powerful unknown group of Origins spellbound all Alderwolves within the confines of the Forest walls, never to leave. The unknown Origins thought the Alderwolves to be guardians of their land. Her gentle and warm father that she had once known seemed lost forever to the Alderwolf Origin.

Aiden reached into his cloak and withdrew her talisman, its etched reptilian eye flared as he held it. "You'll need this," he said, tossing it through the air toward Mabel.

She froze as the cord brushed her fingertips. Shock rooted her in place as she stared at the artefact–retrieved from the false Harrow–now dangling before her.

As she seized the talisman fully, its energy flowed into her, centering on the damage to her body. Warmth blossomed under the bandages as the talisman's magic healed her fractured skull. Then she felt its magic flow down to the torn flesh in her neck. The searing pain faded to a dull ache, then vanished, taking with it any signs of injury.

The pulsing warmth offered a small measure of comfort, yet unease lingered. She searched Aiden's face for answers, but his eyes revealed nothing. With hesitance, Mabel lifted the cord and refastened it around her neck. The talisman settled above her heart, reassuring her that she was not totally alone. She prayed it would help guide and protect her on her journey into the Black Marsh.

The raven swooped in through the open window. It fixed Mabel with an intense gaze, cawing loudly as if to spur her to action.

"What happened to Mother Agnes?" she demanded, her gaze beheld the raven's strange white eyes, an eerie reminder that all of this was because of Agnes in the first place.

"Dead," he murdered the silence with a single word, crimson eyes filled with sorrow.

Mabel staggered back in despair. She clutched at the talisman, the raven had left it in her cell, a gift from Agnes. Had it all been an illusion, a deception?

If Agnes was truly gone, how had Mabel come to possess this artefact? The raven's visit in the dungeon, the talisman's solid weight–it was real, not imagined.

Had her father been the one to help free her and Thomas? It had to have been Aiden. *Has he been working with Mother's familiar?*

The spectral woman in white haunted Mabel's thoughts now–an illusory deceptive Origin that took on the appearance of Mother Agnes. It had to be... if Mother Agnes was dead. But how?

"How... did she–" A daring question started but not finished.

"After you were born, your mother went to the Witch's Grave to perform the Rite of Unmaking to purify your blood, which means she had to make a deal with the Vespers..." Aiden trailed off, hesitance etched onto his face.

"A deal? The Witch's Grave? Vespers? You never told me any of this, Father!" Mabel screamed. "All this time, I've hated my Mother, and she was only trying to free me–"

"–Mabel, I promise answers will come, but right now Thomas is running out of time."

No witch with their wits about them would voluntarily approach the Witch's Grave. The dreaded isle, isolated off the coast of the North Sea, was the notorious lair of the Vespers Origin, whose unending hunger was for the blood of witches. This island, severed from the Mainland, kept the Vespers at bay, preventing them from hunting and devouring the witches in their homeland.

While whispers persisted that the Vespers' venom could purify a witch's blood and break their curse, the danger far overshadowed the potential salvation. The Vespers, more devourers than liberators, preyed upon those witches who ventured into their realm in a desperate quest for cleansing–and in this case, Mother Agnes had fallen victim.

Tears cut streaks through the dirt on Mabel's face. "Then who was it that came to me in the dungeon? Please, Father... I must have answers now!"

Aiden gripped her shoulders as she sobbed. Desperation crept into his voice. "Snap out of it, Mabel!" He spoke urgently, frantically. "Thomas's life hangs by the thinnest of threads. You must find him before the sun sets tomorrow! Once you return, I promise you will have your answers, Mabel, my daughter, listen... listen... to me..."

Swallowing back her doubts, she gave a shaky nod and refocused her thoughts on finding her babe. He was right. She could get her answers later, but right now, every passing second brought Thomas closer to an inevitable unseen demise in the Black Marsh. She had no choice but to bury her questions for now. She sighed and regrouped. "Father, how can you be so certain the Black Marsh Chest has him?"

"Trust me," Aiden uttered.

Mabel shuddered, picturing the Alderwood Origins said to lurk within the marsh. Whispers told of the Ghoul, an emaciated being with sunken eyes, sallow skin stretched over its skeletal frame, and needle-like teeth that hungered insatiably for flesh. It stalked the marsh on all fours like a feral beast, waiting to pounce on anyone foolish enough to venture near. The Weeping Bride, an apparition draped in sodden wedding finery, her face obscured by stringy hair. She floated through the mist, luring victims deeper into the swamp's depths with her mournful sobs. Her wails echoed across the stagnant waters. And the Faceless Ones, spectral beings shrouded in tattered robes, their hooded faces blank voids. They surrounded trespassers, driving them mad with terror as they slowly closed in.

Somewhere in that foetid darkness, amidst the perpetual fog and spike-logged bogs, lay the Cursed Chest holding her dear Thomas. Trees clawed at the grey sky, their twisted branches dripping with Spanish moss. The thick mists swirled with unseen horrors just waiting for fresh victims to wander blindly into their domain. This desolate swampland was home to some of the most vicious and depraved Origins known to walk Alderwood.

No, she could not give in to fear. There was still hope of reaching him before the sacrifice was complete. Mabel collected herself and nodded, shelving her questions about Mother Agnes and the woman in white for now. John would have to wait too.

Not like he's going anywhere, a sadistic thought emerged.

She worried about John, but right now, their son needed her most. That much was true. She would face whatever Origins awaited in the Black Marsh to rescue Thomas or die trying. The choices were clear–venture into the swampland and brave its horrors or lose her babe forever.

Mabel clung to the talisman, feeling its power flowing in tune with her heartbeat. The artefact had shielded her from much of Alderwood's Origins, but now it must help her retrieve her son from the Black Marsh.

She prepared for the unknown threats ahead. She strapped on her trusted longbow with her last arrow and sheathed her dagger. Laced sturdy boots that Aiden had provided for her. Lastly she organised provisions she had found around the cottage and placed them into her satchel—hard bread, dried meat, apples, skins of water, and the hare the raven had gifted her.

Aiden appeared in the doorway, resignation etched on his face. Wordlessly he held out the sword, its razor-sharp blade stained with Accursed blood.

"You'll need this where you're going," he rasped, his gaze carrying notes of shame. Mabel accepted the heavy weapon and belted it on. "I wish I could join you, daughter," but they both knew that Alderwolves were spellbound to the forest.

She met Aiden's eyes and nodded, hating but understanding that she had to face this journey alone.

~*~

The sun hovered low on the horizon as Mabel and Aiden emerged from the dark cloud of the Alderwood Forest. Dusky purples and burnt orange hues bathed the rugged landscape ahead in evening light. They had reached the forest's edge, the outskirts of the Alderwood Mainland unfolded before them.

Mabel gazed out at the terrain, taking in the details. In the distance stood Alderwood Castle, looking almost inviting now compared to the unknown threats ahead. Far beyond the castle lay the Black Marsh.

Aiden placed a hand on her shoulder, sharing a long silence with Mabel. She met his gaze and gave a small nod, steadying her nerves. Aiden longed to join her, to continue assisting his daughter, she realised that now. It was too bad that the Alderwolf curse forbade it.

The raven swooped down to perch nearby. Mabel had thought she would brave the darkness alone, but the raven's presence steeled her spirit.

Mabel tightened her grip on the talisman, its warmth and magic fortifying her blood with strength. With the raven overhead and her weapons close, she was as prepared as she could be. But fear still gnawed within.

Sensing her dread, Aiden murmured, "Remember you are the daughter of the Great Enchantress, Mother Agnes."

The sun disappeared below the horizon. It was time. Mabel embraced her father, his burning eyes reminding her that she would never be forsaken. Then she drew her hood up and strode forth into the Alderwood Mainland, resolutely facing the unknown.

With the raven circling overhead, Mabel moved across the open landscape. The talisman pulsed warmly on her chest, her weapons providing small comfort. She quickened her pace, focused on the castle and marsh beyond. Somewhere ahead hid Thomas, his young life threatening to be cut short. The thought made her blood run cold. She would find him, no matter the cost.

From the forest eaves, two figures watched Mabel depart alone into the deepening dusk. In one spot, Aiden, his burning crimson eyes filled with faith in his daughter. In another, Constable Harrow, his remaining deep blue eye gleaming with hatred, teeth bared in a grin. She shuddered, sensing the evil gazing after her.

Why is he letting me go?

Harrow was one of her greatest fears, the tormentor who had stolen Thomas time and again. Though, she could not dwell on him now.

For in this very moment, the thought of Thomas being sacrificed to the Black Marsh Origins scared her more than any torment Harrow could have ever inflicted upon her. At least with Harrow, Thomas lived unscathed, but the Origins in the Black Marsh would devour him on sight.

She marched on through the twilight, tightening her hold on the talisman. Thomas' cries had long echoed all around Alderwood. Now only silence remained, more terrifying than any scream. At least his wails meant he was still alive. Mabel quickened her pace, desperate to hear her babe's voice again. She plunged into the darkness, guided by the memory of that cry heard around Alderwood.

To Be Continued

Chapter One: The Cry Heard Around Alderwood

Thank You For Reading

My spine-tingling friends,

You've braved the bone-chilling tale of Alderwood's first origin and lived to read these final words. But the true terror has only begun.

Like any thrilling horror franchise, Alderwood must spread its roots across screens and pages so its petrifying aura can haunt you always. But nightmare realms aren't cheap. As a humble horrorsmith, I can only handcraft so many scares alone.

That's where you creeps come in. For less than the price of a brown sugar oatmilk shaken espresso at Starbucks—my drink of choice, and actually that's more expensive because I add an extra shot of espresso with a pump of vanilla, sweet cream cold foam and cinnamon dolce topping, don't judge me—you can unlock the next phase for the Alderwood Origins. Just $4.99 a month on Patreon gives me the adrenaline I need to bring this franchise to its maximal, multi-platform potential. Or you could just actually buy me a brown sugar oatmilk shaken espresso with an extra shot of espresso, a vanilla pump, sweet cream cold foam and cinnamon dolce topping. That helps, too, but I assure you it is also more expensive.

With your support, we'll plunge deeper into fresh books, games, films, merch and many more experiences. Just point your phone camera here for a shortcut to my Patreon, unless you're too scared to face what comes next...